The English Lieutenant's Lady

AVA STONE

 Night Shift Publishing

AVA STONE

Copyright © 2012 Author Name

All rights reserved.

ISBN: 1517271142
ISBN-13: 978-1517271145

Dedication

For my brothers ~ Ryan and Nicholas, you are as different as Tristan and Russell. And like Cordie loves her brothers, I love you both dearly and want the very best for each of you. ~ Ava

One

London – June 1815

AFTER all his years spent on one side of the war-torn continent or the other, with only a slight respite the previous year from all the death and destruction, Lieutenant Tristan Avery was *finally* home. *Home*, with all of London's once familiar sights, sounds and, of course, the smell that could only be the Thames.

He glanced across the hired hack at his brother and shook his head. "I wish Philip was here."

Captain Russell Avery agreed with a nod. "Me too. But the surgeon promised Philip would be fine. He won't be too far behind us." Then he smirked. "So, I suppose we'll simply have to make do without his preaching for the next while or so."

Preaching. Russell's euphemism for their childhood friend's stoic, moral nature. "If you'd only behave, he'd have no reason to *suggest* you do otherwise."

Russell laughed. "And what a boring life that would be. No, no, no. I intend to enjoy my return to civilization one pretty woman at a time."

As though Russell had gone without female companionship the last few years. The last few nights was more like it. Still Tristan couldn't help but needle his brother. "So relieved to hear you've decided to end things with the Greywood chit. I lamented having to look upon her during all of our future family gatherings."

Russell's smile faded and he heaved a sigh. "Don't start again. Phoebe is perfectly fine."

"I wouldn't think *perfectly fine* would be all one wanted in a wife," Tristan replied, then he shrugged. "But then I'm not the one getting married." Or the one who'd had his way with more women than he could count all across the continent the last half dozen years either. Well, Tristan *had* enjoyed his fair share of women, but *he* wasn't betrothed. Though in all honesty, Russell hadn't been either until last year.

"Well, I'm not married yet." Russell leaned forward on his bench. "Why don't we stop of at Madam Palmer's for old time's sake?"

Whores so early in the day? Tristan gaped at his brother as though he'd lost his mind. "I would like to see our sister."

Russell dismissed the idea with a wave of his hand. "We can see her any time."

"And our nephew," Tristan continued. "I would like

to see little Julian. Clayworth probably has him reciting lines from the Magna Carta by now."

Russell rolled his eyes. "We were gone less than four months. I'm sure the little imp isn't even out of his bassinet, yet."

Four months, but it felt like four lifetimes. Tristan frowned at his brother, hating that Russell had a point. Still, they had yet to lay eyes on the infant, born during this last campaign. He'd missed so much in his absence. He missed London. He missed his dear sister. He missed… everything. "Do what you like," he muttered. After all, Russell would do what he wanted anyway, no matter what Tristan thought about it. "But I am heading into Clayworth House, and I'm not going to let Cordie or her little bundle out of my sight all day."

"Well, that sounds perfectly dreadful." Russell yawned as though the subject bored him immensely. "But you can take my bag with you, I'll be otherwise occupied." He closed his eyes and leaned against the shabby squabs. "I plan to be welcomed home in an altogether different fashion."

"Madam Palmer's?" Tristan asked, even though he knew the answer.

A rakish grin settled on Russell's lips. "I have missed English girls."

Yet they'd only been gone less than four months, and he'd had plenty of foreign girls to tide him over in the meantime. Before Tristan could say as much, the hack jerked to a stop. Tristan smiled as the familiar sight of their sister's home on Hertford Street appeared through the window. He tossed open the door and bounded out onto the walk.

"Toss me both bags, will you?" he called to the driver.

"What about the captain?"

Tristan shook his head. "He'll get your fare. He's headed to Covent Garden."

The driver's brow lifted in surprise, then he snorted as though the situation was no matter to him. A moment later he tossed both bags to Tristan, tipped his hat in farewell, and urged his pair of bays back toward Park Lane.

Tristan slung both bags over his left shoulder and climbed the steps to Clayworth House. The door opened before he could knock and Higgins, his sister's usually stoic butler, beamed at him.

"Lieutenant, you're home!" the servant gushed as he held the door wide. "Lady Clayworth will be so relieved to see you!"

Tristan stepped over the threshold and lowered both bags to the marble floor. "I will be happy to see her too, Higgins. Do tell me she's here."

"Of course, sir, of course. Right in there." The butler gestured to the formal green parlor, directly to Tristan's right. "Shall I announce you?"

"No." Tristan shook his head. "I think I'll surprise her."

"Very good, Lieutenant. I'll have you put in your usual room." Higgins glanced at the pair of bags at Tristan's feet. "Is Captain Avery with you as well?"

"He'll be along soon, I'm sure," Tristan replied as he made his way to the parlor entrance. Just as he stepped over the threshold, a stream of giggles reached his ears. Damn it, Cordie wasn't alone. Even worse, he knew *that* giggle.

But before he had time to think on it, Cordie spotted him. She squealed, leapt off the settee, and raced across the parlor, throwing her arms around his neck. "Oh, Tris!" Her hold tightened around him. "I've never been so glad to see anyone," she whispered, just for his ears.

Tristan held her close, so very relieved to be home. He kissed Cordie's cheek, then set her away from him so he could look her over. "Motherhood agrees with you." And truly she did look more radiant than ever.

"Oh!" Cordie beamed at him. "Julian is sleeping, but I can't wait for you to see him."

"I could peek in the nursery," Tristan suggested.

But his sister shook her head, her dark brown curls swaying with the movement. "You'll wake him and then he'll be fussy. And I want you to see him at his most charming."

Tristan was certain the child could scream his lungs out and he'd still find the tiny baron charming. He glanced over his sister's shoulder and found Miss Phoebe Greywood, her hands folded in front of her, standing beside a high-back chair. "Miss Greywood," he said curtly, because he had to say something.

A forced smile settled on her face as she met his gaze. "Lieutenant," she returned. "So glad you've returned home safely."

The little liar. She'd have been just as happy if Tristan had fallen to his death in Belgium. They'd never cared for each other, but she seemed to be making an effort at least. "Thank you. You are looking lovely."

That at least was the truth. Phoebe Greywood might annoy him at every turn, but she was lovely. Rich auburn hair piled high on her head with delicate tendrils framing her heart-shaped face. Pretty azure eyes that twinkled when she was happy, not that she was generally happy in Tristan's presence, but he'd seen her often enough with Russell. And an enchanting smile that lit her countenance, making her seem the cheeriest of girls.

"Thank you, sir. Is…" Miss Greywood cleared her throat. "Is Captain Avery with you?"

Tristan shook his head. "Not at the present."

"Where *is* Russell?" Cordie asked, a slight tone of petulance to her voice.

Presently? About to get his knob polished, if Tristan had to wager a guess, not that he could say as much to his sister or his brother's intended. His eyes flashed again to Phoebe Greywood. She looked so hopeful, so… innocent. Poor girl. She had no idea what she was truly in for after she married Russell. Her days of wondering where the scoundrel captain was were just beginning. "He had something to attend to. I'm certain he'll be along as soon as he can." Then he turned his attention back to his sister. "But Philip…"

The color drained from Cordie's face. "Oh, no, Tris! Tell me he's all right."

Tristan winced a bit. "He'll live," he stressed the word. "He took a ball and a bayonet. His leg is bad, I won't lie to you, but he's getting stronger every day."

"Oh, good heavens." Cordie touched a hand to her heart. "They didn't take his leg?"

"No," Tristan assured her. "The surgeon says he'll have to use a cane the rest of his days, but he'll walk again."

Relief settled across Cordie's features, but she still looked slightly pained. "The poor man."

Indeed. Tristan agreed with a nod. "I still don't think it comes close to the pain in his heart though."

His sister heaved a sigh. "Let's not dredge that back up. Livvie never meant to hurt him and what's done is done."

Tristan shrugged. "I'm not dredging anything up. I'm just worried about him. If you get the chance to see him when he returns, I'd like to hear your thoughts on the matter."

Cordie nodded, then her face lit up with a smile once again. "Oh, Tris. I'm so glad to see you whole and hale."

And though Tristan would like to spend the afternoon reminiscing with his dear sister, he'd really rather not spend any more time than was necessary in Phoebe Greywood's presence. He felt slightly dirty lying to her about his brother's whereabouts, and he'd rather not suffer the feeling the rest of the day. "Is Clayworth in? Or is he at his club?"

Cordie gestured to the corridor. "He's in his study. Do you want me to find you when Julian awakes?"

Tristan flashed her a grin. "I would be quite sore with you if you didn't."

Two

PHOEBE Greywood breathed a sigh of relief when Lieutenant Avery left the parlor in search of his brother-in-law. Their interactions had always been strained. After all, the brute *had* threatened to horsewhip her the very first night they'd met if she didn't betray Cordie's friendship and divulge her whereabouts. How in the world Cordie adored the boorish man above all of her other brothers, Phoebe had no idea.

She dropped back into the high-back chair she had been seated in before Lieutenant Avery arrived and frowned at her friend. "Did he seem evasive to you? About Captain Avery? Do you think everything is all right?"

Cordie shook her head. "Russell probably had some business to attend to. I wouldn't worry about him." Then she resumed her spot on the settee and grinned. "So good to have them both home. I'll have to send a note to Livvie. She can add them to her numbers for tomorrow night."

"I don't know that Mother will let me attend the soiree." Though their friend Olivia was a duchess, she did have a tarnished name. Or rather she'd adopted a tarnished name after her rather hasty union to one of the most scandalous men in all of England.

Cordie's back straightened and a familiar expression of indignation flashed in her eyes. "And why not?" she clipped out, even though she very well knew the reason.

"Cordie," Phoebe sighed, "you have the freedom you always wanted, but I don't have mine yet. No matter how much I adore Olivia, Mother still worries for my reputation."

"You will be married soon. Your fiancé will be in attendance as will, I'm certain, two of your uncles." She heaved a sigh of her own. "Livvie needs our support, Phoebe. We're all she has."

It was sad. Olivia had once been a lady with the most pristine of reputations until the wicked Duke of Kelfield had crossed her path. There was a lesson in that. If one married a reprobate—even if you loved him madly—you might not weather the storm, socially speaking.

"I'll see what I can do," Phoebe promised. Then an image of Russell Avery, handsome hero in his regimentals, flashed in her mind. She couldn't wait to see him again, to kiss him once more. She'd have to make her mother see reason. "I'll pout and throw a temper tantrum since it's been so long since I've seen your brother. I'll even cry if I have to, but I'll manage it somehow."

A wry smile lit Cordie's face. "I have complete faith

that you'll emerge victorious, and while you're scheming to get your way, you must pressure Russell to set a date. The sooner you're my sister, the happier I'll be."

"So will I."

After two Seasons, Phoebe was quite ready to marry her captain and settle into a quiet, domestic bliss. Unfortunately there were two hurdles to her happiness with Russell Avery. The first was his mother, and while a good number of wives didn't get along with their mothers-in-law, Phoebe had seen firsthand the violence Lady Avery was capable of. She'd never forget Cordie's battered body after her mother had reprimanded her the previous year.

Russell's second flaw was his devotion to Lieutenant Avery. They were closer than most brothers, or at least they seemed to be. Of course, that was probably to be expected as they had served alongside each other in battle in addition to being related by blood. Still, it didn't make Phoebe particularly happy. If she could just talk the captain into settling near her parents in Norfolk. Grandpapa had promised her Fairweather Cottage if she wanted it…

An idea occurred to Phoebe. "It is fortuitous that Russell has returned before we've left for Malvern Hall, isn't it? Do you think I could persuade him to come spend the summer with us in Norfolk?"

"It probably won't even take pouting or throwing a temper tantrum." Cordie laughed.

Someone cleared his throat just inside the threshold, drawing both ladies' attention. Higgins nodded at the countess. "Young Lord Bayhurst has awoken from his nap, my lady."

Cordie's grin beamed. "Thank you, Higgins." She turned her attention to Phoebe. "Tristan will be so thrilled. Do excuse me, will you?"

Phoebe nodded. "Of course, of course." And as her friend left the parlor, a pang of want circled Phoebe's heart. How she'd love to hold a little bundle of her own in her arms and kiss his fingers and toes and dote upon him. Phoebe heaved a sigh, her head spinning over and over with two thoughts. One – now that Russell was home, he needed to finally agree to a wedding date. And two – just as soon as they were married they needed to start their family…

Family. What if the something Russell had to attend to was visiting Phoebe and her family? It would be just like her dear fiancé to head straight for Greywood House to attend her upon his return, and it would be just like Tristan Avery to keep that information from her. Odious man. Tristan, not Russell.

The more the thought lingered in Phoebe's mind, the more she was certain that Russell *must* be at her home waiting patiently for her. So she quickly rose from her spot and tugged on the bell pull so Higgins would call for her coach.

"He should only be a few weeks behind us," Tristan said, leaning back in his chair in front of the Earl of Clayworth's desk.

"Poor man." Clayworth frowned. "I know his only want was to retire to Leverton Park. To see to his estate, walk his grounds."

"He'll be able to walk," Tristan replied, and hoped it

was true. But Philip was doggedly determined about whatever he set his mind on, and that knowledge brought Tristan a bit of relief. "Just with a cane," he added softly, which wasn't so bad when one considered the alternative.

Before the earl could reply, Cordie breezed into the study, a tiny little bundle wrapped in white muslin in her arms. Tristan and Clayworth both rose from their spots. "Here he is," the countess cooed. "Julian, you will adore your Uncle Tristan. He will be your favorite uncle, I'm sure."

Tristan crossed the floor to his sister and her child. The little fellow blinked dark blue eyes at Tristan and seemed to assess him in a most studious manner. "Don't you look like your father?" he said, and caressed the infant's cheek with the pad of his thumb.

"Indeed," Cordie gushed. "Brendan will soon have to relinquish the title of Lord Adonis to his son."

Clayworth snorted. "Ridiculous moniker," he mumbled under his breath.

Tristan couldn't help but laugh. "There are worse things one can be called, you can trust me on that." After all, he was fairly certain he and his brothers had been called much more unflattering things over the years. *Much* more unflattering.

"Well," Cordie said with a smile, "tomorrow night at Olivia's soiree, no one will call you anything but that handsome Lieutenant Avery."

"Olivia's soiree?" Tristan frowned at his sister. She couldn't be serious. "Seems a disloyal thing to do to Philip, especially at the moment."

Cordie glanced back at her son and bounced him a

bit. "Your uncle is being difficult, my sweet boy. He forgets that Livvie has been his friend just as long as Philip has."

"Cor," Tristan grumbled.

But she paid him no attention and continued cooing to her child. "He doesn't realize how terribly Livvie's been treated while he's been away being a hero, how important it would be for her friends to support her."

"Fine." Tristan heaved a sigh. He'd learned long ago that it was pointless to argue with his sister. She'd win in the end, anyway; she always did. "I'll be wherever you want me to be."

Cordie grinned and kissed her son's brow. "See, my sweet boy, I knew he'd see reason." Then she glanced back at Tristan. "And I promise you, Kelfield isn't nearly as wicked as you think."

"Supporting Olivia is one thing. I'll stop at praising her husband, if you don't mind."

Three

"Olivia's done rather well for herself," Tristan mumbled to Russell as they trailed behind their sister and Clayworth, into the Duke of Kelfield's opulent drawing room, adorned in dark blue with golden accents and containing a chandelier that could easily light entire southern coast of France. Tristan let his gaze trail over the room, which was sparsely populated with His Grace's closest friends.

Russell rolled his eyes. "She's in love with him," he said, mocking Cordie's imperious tone. "Or so I've been told a half dozen times until I finally relented." They breezed past a couple of guests, staying close to the edge of the room. "Not sure how Clayworth lives with her."

At that, Tristan couldn't help but smile. "He's in love with her." Then he shook his head. "I don't know why you held for out so long, anyway. You knew she'd win in the end."

Russell shrugged. "I suppose after Quatre Bras and Waterloo, I like to think I can win every now and then."

"Against the French, yes." Tristan chuckled. "Against our sister, never." But he stopped laughing when Russell's face suddenly lost all its color. "What's wrong?"

"Phoebe," Russell muttered so low only Tristan could hear him in their corner.

Tristan's gaze flashed across the room to find the lovely Miss Greywood standing beside her brother and her uncle, Lord Carteret. There was no reason for Russell to lose his pallor. If anything, Phoebe Greywood looked more radiant than she had before they'd left for the continent earlier in the year. Usually a pretty girl would make Russell salivate, not look as though he was going to cast up his accounts. "What about her?"

Russell glared at Tristan out of the corner of his eye. "Did you know she would be here?"

"Why would I?" He certainly wasn't the girl's confidante. He hadn't even given Phoebe Greywood another thought since the previous afternoon. "Although, she is one of Olivia's few remaining friends, so I can see why she—" He smiled his widest as Olivia, the Duchess of Kelfield, appeared before them. "Your Grace!" Tristan bowed his head.

"Your Grace," Russell echoed a half second later.

The duchess' charming smile lit the room as she looked from Tristan to Russell and back again. "Really? I've known you entirely too long for such formalities. In fact, I'm fairly certain one of you is responsible for a toad I found under my counterpane many, many years ago."

"Ahh, but you weren't a duchess then." Russell winked at her.

Olivia leaned forward and kissed Russell's cheek, then did the same to Tristan. "I am so glad to see you both home and unharmed."

Briefly, Tristan wondered if Olivia knew of Philip's injuries, but pushed the thought aside. Now would not be the time to mention the situation. It might never be the time. No good would come of it, after all. "And you are looking lovely, Livvie."

A rakish grin settled on Russell's face, the one he used whenever he thought to charm a woman. "Though no lady is as lovely as my dear Miss Greywood," he said in his most silky voice, and that was when Tristan realized Phoebe and her brother Matthew had crossed the room and were standing directly behind Olivia.

As though on cue, Miss Greywood blushed, batted her eyes at Russell and giggled. Tristan barely suppressed a groan. Why did fairly intelligent women always fall prey to Russell's cultivated charm? Couldn't any of them see his brother for the accomplished lothario he truly was? Insincere and practiced?

Olivia's gaze locked with Tristan's, and her brow rose slightly as though she'd heard his inner thoughts and agreed completely. Then again, *she* was married to an accomplished lothario herself. She could probably spot one a mile away.

"Cordie tells me Kelfield has an extensive library," Tristan began, though his sister had told him no such thing.

The duchess smiled at him. "You just arrived, Tris. Are you in need of escaping my soiree already?"

Tristan cringed just a bit. "It's been a while since anyone has expected me to make polite conversation in drawing rooms. I'm completely out of practice."

Olivia nodded as though that made perfect sense to her. "If you find you need a respite, you are welcome to peruse Alex's library, if you'd like."

"We'll never see him again with that offer." Russell slapped a hand to Tristan's back. "He's always been quite happy to escape inside the pages of one book or another."

"A learned man is an attractive one," Olivia countered, blessed lady that she was.

Russell conceded her point with a shrug. "I'll take your word for that, Livvie. Though I prefer to surround myself with living, breathing people. Don't you, my dear?"

"I suppose it depends on the living, breathing people in question, Captain." Phoebe Greywood's voice sounded all breathy as she spoke. Then she blushed anew when he met her gaze. "I am so relieved to find you safe and sound and finally home."

Russell inclined his head as though to acknowledge her words. "As I am relieved to find you looking so well, my dear." Charm exuded from him as he stepped forward, captured the girl's hand, and brushed his lips across her knuckles. "You don't know how often I conjured up your face in my mind while I was away."

"And how happy I am you've returned. Might I impose upon you to take a turn about the room with me?" she asked. "I believe we have much to discuss."

Before her last words were even out of her mouth, Russell tucked her hand in the crook of his arm and began to lead her away from Tristan and Olivia. "Spending time with you would never be an imposition."

That Tristan highly doubted, not that he could say as much. As soon as the pair was out of earshot, Tristan turned his attention to Matthew Greywood, and he shook the young man's hand. "It has been an age, Greywood. You're looking well."

Olivia smiled at the pair and then said, "Excuse me, will you? I must speak with your sister for a moment," before making a direct path to Cordie's side.

Matthew Greywood cleared his throat. "Is he playing her for a fool?" he asked as Russell led Phoebe toward the far wall.

"A fool?" Tristan echoed. Phoebe didn't really need any help in that regard, in his opinion. She often had a difficult time remaining upright, after all.

The young man nodded, keeping his eye on his sister. "She refused to leave the house today, convinced Captain Avery would make an appearance."

Which, of course, he didn't do. Damn it. The last spot Tristan wanted to find himself in was defending Russell or making excuses for him. He shrugged. "My brother keeps his own counsel. Excuse me, will you? I think I'd like to glance around Kelfield's library after all."

※

Finally! Finally, Phoebe had Russell Avery exactly where she wanted him. Namely, by her side and giving her his undivided attention. Four months had never crawled by so slowly as they had when he was gone.

"I had hoped to see you yesterday," she said softly as they strolled past the Staveleys and Beckfords.

"Yesterday?" He blinked innocently at her as though he didn't understand why she would think such a thing.

Phoebe gulped, hoping to find the right words. She wasn't trying to berate him, just curious why he hadn't yet come Greywood House. "I—Well, when I saw Lieutenant Avery yesterday, I thought you might have come to see me."

Russell's charming smile retuned and he drew her closer to him. "Yesterday," he continued smoothly, "I had business at Whitehall. But I will call on you tomorrow, my dear."

Tomorrow. "I'll look forward to it," she said softly. And though a smile was on her face, her heart couldn't help but ache. After all, he hadn't come *yesterday* and he hadn't come *today*. Why hadn't he sought her out since his arrival? Didn't he want to see her? Shouldn't he have rushed to her door the way Philip Moore had rushed to Livvie's last year? Was it possible Russell's affection for her had faded while he was away? Or had Lieutenant Avery finally been successful at souring the captain against her?

He looked down at her with his startlingly green eyes and said, "Are you all right, my dear?"

Not in the least. She was a ninny. Why should she let such thoughts plague her? Russell was finally home and they would be married just as soon as it could be arranged. Letting her mind conjure up all manner of unpleasantness wouldn't serve her. "I'm fine," she muttered. Then she forced another smile to her face and said, "Papa wanted…or rather, I'd hoped I could persuade you to come to Malvern Hall this summer."

Russell shook his head. "I can probably get the time

to visit… at some point."

Visit? At some point? Every time he spoke, it was like a dagger to Phoebe's chest. "I had hoped it wouldn't just be for a visit, Captain. We have a wedding to plan and don't you think we should reacquaint ourselves with each other first?"

He stopped mid-step and spun her to face him. "What is this about, Phoebe?"

"It's about us getting on with our lives. Starting our lives. Together." Did he not see that?

Russell frowned just a bit. "There's no rush, my dear. We have the rest of our lives, you know."

She blinked at him. How was it possible they saw the situation so differently?

"Besides," he continued, "Tristan and I will be opening Avery House soon."

"But the Season has ended," she stressed, afraid that she sounded the tiniest bit petulant, but there was nothing for it. Didn't he want to see her? "I'm leaving for Norfolk in but a few days."

"I will try to see you before you depart."

Before she departed? "I thought you said tomorrow." Heavens, was the room starting to spin?

"Of course, of course," he assured her. "I'll call on you tomorrow, and I will try to make it to Malvern Hall this summer so we can reacquaint ourselves, as you say."

He would *try*? Try to make the day and a half journey after he'd been across the channel for months? How magnanimous! Phoebe didn't think she'd hated any word as much as she abhorred 'try' at that moment. Had he *tried* to see her yesterday or even today and failed in those endeavors?

"Well, I do hope you'll be *successful* in your tries, sir." She hated the waspish sound in her voice, but couldn't help it. She'd been so relieved, so thrilled that he'd returned home from the battlefield, but he didn't appear to return even a fraction of her elation.

She released her hold on his arm and turned on her heel.

"Phoebe," he called after her.

But she didn't turn around. If she did, he'd see the tears she was blinking back, and that would never do.

Four

WHO would have thought Kelfield owned a collection of books on dog breeds? Must have been quite a surprise to learn Livvie was deathly afraid of the creatures. Tristan suppressed a smile just as a splash of green crossed in front of the library door, quickly followed by a very feminine and a very familiar yelp. He dropped the book on Norfolk Spaniels on the closest table and bolted into the corridor.

In the middle of the hallway, Phoebe Greywood lay face down in a pool of green silk, her round little bottom pointing upward. Was it possible she'd become even less graceful while he was away?

Tristan heaved a beleaguered sigh. "Are you all right?" he asked as he strode toward her and held out his hand in assistance.

When she looked up at him, his heart clenched at the sight. Tears streamed down her face, her lip trembled, and a blush crept up her neck. Poor girl looked mortified.

Dear God. Tristan sunk down to his haunches to see her better. "Are you hurt?"

She shook her head and swiped at her cheeks with the back of her gloves.

"Here." He offered her a handkerchief, which she regarded as Cleopatra might an approaching asp. "It's just a handkerchief, Miss Greywood."

She sniffed indignantly, then snatched the piece of cloth from him. "Th-thank you." She dabbed at her eyes.

Tristan pushed back to his feet and once again offered the girl his hand. "Come on. Let me help you up."

She placed her dainty hand in his and allowed him to pull her back to her feet. Her eyes lowered to the floor and she tried to push Tristan's handkerchief back in his hand, but he stepped backward.

"You keep it," he said.

She sniffed again, still refusing to meet his eyes.

Tristan should have left her in the corridor. He should have turned around and returned to the drawing room with the others. But there was something about her frailty in that moment. Something about the sagging of her shoulders. He took a step forward and tipped her chin up with a crooked finger so she'd have to meet his eyes. The sadness in the azure depths that stared back at him nearly stole his breath. In an instant he was overcome with the desire to wrap his arms around her and promise that everything would be all right. That he'd make certain she was all right.

He cleared his throat in an attempt to shake himself

from the spell of her gaze. "Come now, Miss Greywood, you've taken worse spills," he said lightheartedly. He'd *seen* her take worse spills. Newborn fouls had more grace than she did at times.

Her face flamed anew, and she took a step backwards. "It's hardly gentlemanly to say such a thing."

"Ah." He quirked her a grin. "But I'm not a gentleman." Or at least she'd told him that more than a dozen times in the past.

"Truer words were never spoken, you brute," she muttered, which only made Tristan toss back his head and laugh.

"I am so relieved you are back to your former self, Miss Greywood."

"I beg your pardon?"

He shook his head. "You were so polite yesterday. I barely recognized you. So glad to know the world hasn't shifted on its axis during my absence."

Her lips twitched as though she had the urge to smile but refused to give him that satisfaction.

"Go on," he prodded. "I am rather amusing. It's all right to smile."

An unladylike snort escaped her, but then she did flash a grin at him. "You are arrogant, Lieutenant."

Tristan shrugged. "Avery curse, I'm afraid. We all have a touch of it."

And at that her face fell once more and her lip quivered anew. What the devil?

"Miss Greywood, what is the matter?"

But she shook her head and stubbornly said nothing. Something had happened however, and for some reason

Tristan felt driven to discover what it was.

"Let's escape into the library, shall we?" He offered her his arm, and surprisingly, she took it. A bolt of heat shot through him from the contact, which was more than alarming.

Why should he feel a sudden pull towards Phoebe Greywood? He didn't even like her. He never had. Tristan mentally shook the thought from his mind. He didn't feel a pull towards Phoebe Greywood. He just hated to see her cry. He hated to see any woman cry. Yes, that must be the explanation.

Tristan directed her into the library and gestured to the book he'd been thumbing through before she fell. "Kelfield has volumes upon volumes on dog breeding."

"The dowager duchess breeds sheep dogs."

"Oh, dear God." Tristan failed to contain a laugh.

"I can't imagine what is amusing about that."

Tristan shook his head. "Olivia is terrified of dogs, ever since she was a child and was attacked by one."

"I hardly find that something to laugh about." She looked at him as though he truly was the brute she'd accused him of being moments ago.

"I'm not laughing about that," he tried to explain. "I'm laughing at the irony of her mother-in-law breeding dogs."

"Oh, well, that's all right then, I suppose." Phoebe spun away from him but caught her foot in the hem of her gown, and she stumbled forward. A startled gasp escaped her, but she did manage to find her footing and keep from tumbling to the ground once more.

Dear God, she was clumsy. He couldn't help but smile, which of course she noticed.

She glared at him at the same time she as lifted her hem to avoid tripping on it again and walked further into the library. "What were you doing in here, anyway?"

Some imp on Tristan's shoulder urged him to say, "I was looking to see if Kelfield had any books on Ancient Rome."

She glanced over her shoulder at him, her eyes narrowed. Oh, yes, she remembered that first conversation they'd ever had. He could see it clearly in her countenance. "Ancient Rome?"

Holding back a smirk, he parroted back her words to him from that long ago exchange, "I find the era fascinating."

"And I'm Julius Caesar," she returned, although much softer than he'd said those very words to her the previous year.

Tristan let his smile break as he closed the distance between them. "You look so much more like a Calpurnia, I would think." He leaned his hip against the long wooden table and braced his hands on the edges.

Miss Greywood's brows rose in amusement. "Calpurnia? Is that the best you can do? I would think Aphrodite would be more complimentary."

Tristan shrugged. "But Aphrodite was a blonde and your hair is so much more rich in color."

"Are you flirting with me, Lieutenant Avery?" She dropped onto a divan against the wall and folded her arms beneath her breasts, lifting the lovely mounds higher in her gown. How had ne never noticed how utterly delightful her breasts looked before now?

"Distracting you from whatever it was that sent you

fleeing down the corridor. Is it working?" He was certainly distracted. But for God's sake, she was his brother's fiancée. What was wrong with him?

She heaved a sigh. "I suppose I thought Russell would return home, and we'd rush right into getting our lives back in order, and we'd pick up where we left off."

So Russ was responsible for her fragile state, was he? Tristan supposed he shouldn't be surprised. "We've seen a lot, Miss Greywood. We've endured a lot. I'm sure he just needs time to readjust to life before leaping into anything at the moment." Perhaps after Russ had bedded half of London, he'd be ready to slow down and pay attention to his fiancée. And perhaps Wellington would declare his undying love for Napoleon Bonaparte.

Phoebe Greywood's long lashes brushed the top of her cheeks, then she pierced him with her azure gaze. "Why are you being nice to me, Lieutenant?"

"Maybe I've had enough battles to last me a lifetime. Shall we call a truce?"

"Perhaps a temporary one," she conceded.

Tristan pushed away from the table and dropped onto the divan beside her. "Word of advice, then, Miss Greywood?" he said, as her heavenly lilac scent invaded his senses. He'd never thought of lilac as enticing until now.

"Advice?" she echoed.

"About my brother." Then Tristan winced. What he was about to offer wasn't the most loyal suggestion, at least as far as his brother went, but it was most definitely in her best interest. "While Russ takes his time readjusting to society, I think you should ask yourself if he's truly the man for you."

Her face turned a bit pink. "I beg your pardon?"

"I mean," he continued, "he *did* send you crying down the corridor. Is that what you want the rest of your days? I know he needs time to settle back into society, but—"

Before he could finish his statement, her hand connected with his cheek. Tristan's teeth rattled in his head. So much for their truce.

"How dare you?" she spat, all fire and indignation. "I know you never approved of me, but—"

"I'm only trying to help," Tristan protested. And he was. Russell and Phoebe Greywood would never suit. And they'd be miserably stuck with each other all their days if she didn't come to her senses.

Miss Greywood snorted, then started to rise, but Tristan tugged her hand until she landed back on the divan.

"Unhand me," she ground out.

He relinquished his hold on her hand. Clearly she was in no mood to listen to reason this evening. He shouldn't have been surprised by that. She had never seemed the sort who would listen to reason. Why had he even bothered? "Allow me to storm out, Miss Greywood. I don't think there's any danger of *me* falling on *my* face as I quit the room." And with that he rose to his feet and escaped into the safety of the corridor.

Five

OH! Phoebe hated him. Horrid man. Trying to get her to question her devotion to Russell!

She folded her arms and wished Tristan Avery to the devil as he strode from the room. *There's no danger of me falling on my face as I quit the room*. Oh, she'd love to watch him fall on his face once. Just once. After all, he'd always found her spills more than amusing, hadn't he? It would be quite fitting for the slipper – or boot, rather – to be on the other foot. She wouldn't even try to suppress a grin should he tumble to the ground. Blackhearted scoundrel.

"Phoeb?" Her brother Matthew stood on the threshold, his brow creased in a frown. "Are you all right?"

She was far from all right, but she couldn't admit as much to Matthew. She wouldn't even know what to say. *Tristan Avery was horrid to me!* That would make her sound like a petulant child. So she shrugged instead. "Just tired."

Matthew snorted as he stepped into the library and closed the distance between them. "Lieutenant Avery nearly knocked me to the floor in his haste just now. Did you two quarrel again?"

"Every conversation with Lieutenant Avery is a quarrel."

Finally in front of her, Matthew heaved a sigh. "Why must the Avery brothers vex you? That is *my* role as your brother, and I really don't appreciate the pair of them usurping my position."

Begrudgingly, Phoebe smiled at her brother. He did love to needle her, after all. "And you do such a wonderful job of it most of the time, Matt."

"I don't like to brag," he replied as he lifted his hand to her. "Mother's wondering where you are."

Phoebe winced. "Can't you put her off?"

"Normally, but since Russell Avery made his own escape, I think she's worried the two of you were hiding somewhere together."

"Captain Avery's gone?" Phoebe's mouth fell open in surprise.

"He mumbled something about Major Moore under his breath as he was leaving." Matthew shrugged. "I don't think anyone else heard him, but I was right by the door."

So Mama thought she was engaging in a *tête-à-tête* with Russell, did she? Phoebe had no idea her mother thought so lowly of her virtue. "I am mildly offended by Mama's opinion of me."

Matthew snorted. "The man did just return from the

continent. And you have spoken of nothing but him for months. I have to admit, I was surprised to discover you spending your time with Tristan Avery instead."

As though she would choose to spend time with that deplorable oaf. Phoebe scowled at her brother. "I fell. He helped me. That was it."

"You?" Matthew chortled. "*You* fell? I don't believe it."

"You can go to the devil," she grumbled, which only made her brother laugh harder.

"I probably will," he agreed good-naturedly. "But in the meantime, Mother awaits." He wiggled his fingers at her.

Phoebe accepted her brother's assistance and allowed him to tug her from the divan, then she slid her hand around his arm and let him lead her back to the drawing room. Still, her mind was a jumble over Russell's departure and his less than warm response to their reunion. On top of all of those unpleasant thoughts, the image of Tristan Avery smirking at her lying in a heap in the middle of the corridor flashed once more in her mind. Blast the man.

―⁂―

Tristan lifted a glass of Madeira to his lips and scanned the room for someone safe to talk to, and his eyes landed on the Duke of Kelfield, who was looking directly at Tristan. Of all the rotten luck. He couldn't cut the man. Not in his own home. So Tristan nodded a greeting and hoped His Grace would leave it at that.

Thankfully, the duke turned his attention to his wife and seemed to get caught up in a conversation with Livvie and the Beckfords. Tristan would have breathed a sigh of relief, but a hand clapped him on the back at that very moment. He glanced over his shoulder to find the one man in the room he despised more than Kelfield. "Haversham," he grumbled.

The Marquess of Haversham's lips curled up in a wicked grin as though he knew exactly how much Tristan detested him. "You seem to have as many friends in the room as I do."

Tristan scoffed. "Do I have so few? I had no idea."

Haversham chuckled, which was slightly annoying as he seemed completely unperturbed by Tristan's jab. "Clayworth can abide me. Surprising you and your brothers still cannot."

"Brothers have a way of holding grudges against men who set out to ruin their sisters."

Haversham nodded as though that made sense to him. "I'll keep that in mind the next time I set out to ruin a girl." Then his smile brightened as he looked across the room. "Tell me, Lieutenant, does a man hold a grudge against his own brother for trying to steal his fiancée away?"

Tristan glanced toward whatever had captured Haversham's notice and heaved a sigh when he realized Phoebe Greywood had re-entered the drawing room. "I have no idea what you're talking about."

"Don't you?" the marquess chuckled again. "I find that hard to believe, Lieutenant. If I was an honorable man, I'd feel it my duty to warn Captain Avery about the *vis-à-vis* I nearly stumbled upon in Kelfield's library."

Tristan's gaze shot back to the infuriating marquess. "Go ahead. He's the one who made her cry. I was simply trying to help, though only God knows why I tried."

That made Haversham laugh even harder. "Oh, I think you know why you tried, Lieutenant. You haven't been gone from civilization that long."

Tristan itched to send the marquess sprawling across the drawing room floor but imagined his sister wouldn't be terribly thrilled with him for doing so. Instead he scowled at the man. "I do not have designs on my brother's intended, if that is what you are suggesting."

Haversham's smirk returned. "You keep telling yourself that, Lieutenant, and perhaps you'll even start to believe it."

"I don't even like the chit," Tristan ground between his teeth.

The marquess agreed with a nod. "And Lady Staveley doesn't like me either." He gestured to the viscountess in question with a tilt of his head. "Yet still, her eyes seek me out even now."

Lady Staveley? Tristan glanced at the lady, only to see her head turn the other direction and her arm slide through her husband's. "That's ridiculous."

"Like often has nothing to do with lust, Avery. Nothing to do with passion or need. That's why it's a deadly sin."

"You're delusional," Tristan scoffed.

He didn't lust after Phoebe Greywood, annoying little piece of baggage that she was. And Lady Staveley was not lusting after Haversham, of all people. The lady was in love with her husband and always had been. Everyone knew that. She was completely devoted to Viscount Staveley. For Haversham to believe otherwise made him a fool.

"Then I'm in good company with you, Lieutenant."

Tristan glanced back where Miss Greywood now stood. Her countenance lit with frivolity as she giggled between Livvie and Cordie. He shook his head as though to shake away all thoughts of the girl. He did *not* lust after Phoebe Greywood. He did not. The idea was ridiculous. Still, if her *décolletage* wasn't quite so tempting, it would be much easier to erase the memory of their encounter in Kelfield's library completely from his mind.

His cheek, however, would remember the sting of her hand for quite some time.

Six

"THAT sounds nice," Phoebe mumbled to Lady Felicity Pierce as they made their way down Rotten Row. Her eyes scanned the path, searching for any potential pitfalls that would send her tumbling to the ground while her mind was still a jumble over her departure for Norfolk the next morning. Following Felicity's often erratic train of thought wasn't the easiest thing to do—not and remain upright in any event. And all of that—every step, every thought—was compounded by her worry over Captain Avery.

"Phoeb!" A slight air of petulance sounded in Felicity's voice. "You're not listening to me at all."

"Of course I am!" Phoebe protested and stopped mid-step to keep from stumbling.

Felicity tilted her golden head to the side, letting her eyes lock with Phoebe's. "Liar."

Phoebe's mouth fell open. "Felicity Pierce!"

"Well, you are." Her friend's green eyes lit with amusement. "I asked your opinion on my sprouting wings and flying home to Prestwick Chase."

Oh, heavens. How had she missed that ludicrous comment? "You did?"

Felicity nodded. "And you said, 'That sounds nice'."

Blast! Phoebe frowned at her friend. "I am sorry, Lissy. My mind was elsewhere. Forgive me?"

Felicity heaved a sigh and linked her arm with Phoebe's, drawing her back among the throng out for a stroll. "He still hasn't called on you?"

"Is it that obvious?" Phoebe hated the whine she heard in her voice.

Felicity shook her head. "You know, growing up, Juliet never had anything good to say about the male of the species—"

"And then she married a notorious rake."

"A reformed one," Felicity corrected with a giggle. "But that wasn't where I was going with this conversation."

"My apologies." Phoebe bit back a smile. "Do make your point, then."

"All I meant to say was that I think Captain Avery embodies every terrible thing Juliet ever said about men." Then she pursed her lips. "I can't even imagine how he sleeps at night. Dishonorable lout."

"Lissy!" Phoebe chastised. "I am going to marry the man."

Felicity snorted at that. "I wouldn't." Then a familiar darkness settled across the girl's features whenever the subject of marriage arose. "Short of death, there's no escape from marrying the wrong man, Phoeb. You can trust me on that score."

Phoebe wasn't certain what Felicity's late husband had done to her friend during their very short marriage. After all, Lissy refused to speak about the situation at all, but whatever had happened must have been awful indeed. "You sound like Lieutenant Avery," she grumbled instead of prying again about the mysterious American.

At that Felicity touched a hand to her heart and feigned insult. "And I thought we were dear friends. How can you compare me to your worst enemy?" Then a mischievous grin lit her face as she seemed to notice someone approaching from the other direction. "Uncle Fin!" she called, her voice filled with cheer.

Phoebe glanced up to find Viscount Carraway approaching them, his brow furrowed in annoyance. "I am not your uncle," the handsome politician said once he was close enough to do so without yelling. And he wasn't, not really.

Felicity only giggled. "Yes, but it is so delightful to needle you, my lord."

"Afternoon, Lord Carraway," Phoebe muttered quietly.

"Afternoon, Miss Greywood." The viscount nodded in greeting before turning his attention back to the blonde. "Have you heard from Edmund recently?" he asked after Felicity's younger half-brother, whose uncle he *did* happen to be.

Felicity shook her head. "Juliet says he must be enjoying this term and has forgotten all about his sisters."

Carraway nodded, though his frown seemed a bit

darker now. "I'll stop in and see him on my way home next week. I'll remind him that dukes should not neglect familial duties."

Felicity's smile only brightened. "Oh, let him enjoy himself, Fin. He has a lifetime of duties ahead of him."

"You're as bad as Juliet with coddling him," he grumbled.

Felicity shrugged. "If you are trying to insult me, Uncle Fin, you shall have to try harder than that."

"I am *not* your uncle," he reminded her again.

"Then you shouldn't act like it," she replied cheekily. "Would you like to join us on our stroll, my lord?"

Carraway shook his head. "Thank you, but I am meeting someone."

"Oh, *someone*." Felicity clapped her hands together. "I do hope whoever she is, she can make you a little less grumpy. Tell me, who are you meeting?"

A beleaguered sigh escaped the viscount as he shook his head once more. "Do try to stay out of trouble, Lissy."

"And miss out on all the fun in life?" she protested, linking her arm with Phoebe's once more and tugging her friend forward, further away from the viscount. "Have a delightful day, Uncle Fin," she called back over her shoulder.

Phoebe couldn't help but laugh. "That poor man," she said, once they were far enough away from Carraway for him to overhear. "I think you delight in torturing him."

Felicity shrugged. "He's too serious by half."

He was entitled to be morose, however. "The love of his life *was* killed."

"She was *my* sister." Felicity heaved a sigh that would have made Carraway proud, had he heard it. "Besides, Georgie would not want him to mope the rest of his days. And it's already been three years." Then she looked back over her shoulder at the viscount once more. "Actually, he's the sort you should have set your cap for, Phoebe."

"Lord Carraway?" She cast her friend a sidelong glance. Had she lost her mind? Nice as Lord Carraway was, Felicity was correct in her estimation of the man. He was too serious by half.

"Well, not him specifically," Felicity amended. "Unless you like the brooding sort, but I meant noble, constant. A man like Carraway wouldn't treat you so shabbily. He would have come to call on you by now. He wouldn't let you go off to Norfolk without seeing you first, without seeing your father. And he wouldn't have vanished from Livvie's soiree the way Captain Avery did. He would be ever present, though perhaps more so than you'd like, now that I think about it."

"And do you find yourself thinking about his lordship on a regular basis?" Phoebe asked, unable to keep from teasing her friend.

"He is often underfoot. Luke and Juliet seem to adore his company." A frown creased Felicity's brow. "Well, there's an Avery man. Just not the one I'd like to give a piece of my mind to."

Phoebe glanced down the path, and her step faltered when she recognized Tristan Avery, out for a stroll with Cordie, pushing a baby carriage. She snorted. A piece of her mind? "I wouldn't give him the time of day."

"Don't argue with him in front of all the *ton*," Felicity

warned.

※※※

"Be nice," Cordie urged under her breath.

Be nice? The last time Tristan was nice to the little piece of baggage, she rattled the teeth in his head. "I'm always nice," he grumbled, cursing his awful luck. All he wanted was to enjoy a nice day in the park with Cordie and his nephew. Why did they have to cross paths with Phoebe Greywood?

His sister shot him a withering glare, so Tristan stood his tallest, glanced toward the pair of ladies that were now before them and forced a smile to his face. "Lady Felicity." He dipped his head in greeting. Then he let his gaze settle on the girl who never failed to exasperate him. "Miss Greywood."

Her blue eyes locked with his and Tristan's breath rushed from his lungs. Dear God, was she somehow making herself more beautiful each time he saw her? Phoebe's auburn tresses trailed over one delicate shoulder, directing his gaze to her tempting *décolletage* he'd only first noticed the other night. Damn it all. Was she torturing him on purpose with her daydress that displayed her charms so nicely?

"Oh!" Phoebe let out a squeal of delight and leaned forward over the baby carriage, smiling at the tiny little baron and allowing Tristan's gaze to take in even more of her charms.

He shifted his trousers.

"Julian! You are precious," Phoebe gushed, her attention solely focused on the baby before her.

The joy that exuded from her as she caressed the boy's cheek made Tristan take a slight step backwards.

He'd never seen her quite so at ease, so – dare he think it – graceful.

"Are you smiling at Aunt Phoebe?" Cordie cooed, which elicited a smile from the baby and the kick of his feet.

"Aww," Phoebe breathed out. Then she glanced back up at Cordie. "He is enchanting."

"You are a countess." Lady Felicity scoffed. "I don't understand why you don't have his nurse take him for a stroll, Cordie."

Phoebe gasped. "Lissy! How can you suggest that?" Her attention returned to the child. "If I had a little bundle like Julian Reese, I'd never let him out of my sight."

And then it hit Tristan, almost like he'd been coshed over the head with an end of a rifle. Phoebe Greywood would have a little bundle like Julian Reese one day. A little bundle sired by *Russell*. Tristan thought he might be ill at the thought, at the idea of Phoebe Greywood raising and adoring Russell's children, when he had an overwhelming desire, in that moment, to see her raise his own brood instead.

Bloody hell! Where the devil had that thought come from? Damn Haversham to hell for planting such ideas in his mind! Tristan's mouth went dry and he took another step backwards, though his head didn't seem any clearer.

"Tris." Cordie touched his arm, bringing him back to the present. "Are you all right? You look pale all of a sudden."

Did he? Tristan wasn't surprised. After all, it wasn't every day a fellow realized he was enamored with his brother's betrothed. How the devil had that happened? He hadn't even liked her last week. In fact, he wasn't sure if he liked her now. But there was something about her that he couldn't shake from his thoughts. Something about the way her face lit with joy as she doted on the baby. Something about the way the breeze lifted her auburn tendrils. Something about the way her slightly parted lips made him want to taste them, to kiss them, to feel them brush across his body.

Dear God, he was losing his mind.

"Tris!" Cordie's voice interrupted his thoughts once again. "Tristan, there's a bench, right over there. Go sit down."

But he shook his head. "I'm fine." Though he was the furthest thing from it. He cleared his throat. "When do you start for Malvern Hall, Miss Greywood?"

"Tomorrow," she replied, frowning at him. "Actually, you do look pale, Lieutenant. Perhaps you should sit a while."

Tomorrow. Thank God. If he didn't have to run into her at every turn, he could get past whatever this madness was.

"It would be nice," Lady Felicity's slightly waspish tone hit his ears, "if Captain Avery would be good enough to call on her before that time, don't you agree, Lieutenant?"

"Lissy!" Phoebe blushed.

"Russell hasn't been by Greywood House?" Cordie's mouth fell open.

No, Russell hadn't called on her. He'd avoided the place as though he'd catch his death if he showed his face on Phoebe's stoop.

"I'm certain he's been busy," Phoebe defended, though it didn't sound as though she believed her own words. So why was she defending the cad then? Russell certainly wasn't deserving of such loyalty.

"Too busy to see his betrothed before she leaves Town?" Cordie muttered. Then she glanced over her shoulder at Tristan. "I haven't seen him either since the two of you opened Avery House. What has he been up to?"

Nothing Tristan would ever admit aloud to any of these women. "He keeps his own council," he repeated his words to Matthew Greywood from the other night. "On second thought, I think I will sit for just a spell," he said and quickly made his escape to the closest bench before his sister could call him back and demand he answer her questions.

Seven

TRISTAN winced as Cordie started for him, pushing the baby carriage toward his bench. At least Phoebe and Lady Felicity had gone on their way. Now if only he could avoid Phoebe as expertly as Russell had managed to until she left for Norfolk, perhaps he could get his mind off the chit.

"I would never think to find such cowardice in a lieutenant of your stature," his sister admonished once she stood before him.

He scowled in response. "You didn't put me in the best position back there," he grumbled. "What should I have done? Actually tell the three of you where Russ spends his days and nights?"

Cordie's pretty face drew up in a frown. "Where does he spend them?" she asked and dropped onto the bench beside Tristan.

Damn. He shouldn't have said that, not to her. But

his thoughts were all out of order this afternoon, thanks to Miss Greywood. "Nowhere I'll ever tell you about."

"That bad, is it?"

Tristan shrugged instead of answering. After all, the best way not to reveal information was to keep one's mouth closed.

Cordie heaved a sigh. "I suppose that's why the two of you opened Avery House, so you wouldn't have to answer to me."

"You have a husband and a child who need your attention, Cor. It's better for us to be somewhere else."

"Somewhere I can't keep an eye on you?"

He snorted. "You are our *younger* sister, Cordie. Just because you're a countess doesn't mean you get to put us on leashes."

"Perhaps Russell needs to wear one," she countered.

Considering his brother's proclivities, Russell had probably enjoyed something along those lines before. "Let's just drop this, shall we?"

Cordie pursed her lips as though she wasn't prepared to drop anything, but then she said, "So, Brendan received a missive today."

"Oh?" Tristan glanced at his sister, suspicious that she'd truly changed the subject so easily.

"A distant cousin has begged for an invitation to Town for his daughter."

The topic sounded innocuous enough. "Cousin?"

"Hmm. It seems this Miss Pritchard has broken an engagement and is in need of a change of scenery."

A broken engagement. The words lifted Tristan's heart just a bit. If only Phoebe Greywood would break *her* engagement, then he wouldn't have to spend the rest of his life watching her bat her pretty eyelashes in Russell's unworthy direction. "Sounds like a smart girl."

Cordie's brow rose in slight amusement. "You sound as cynical as Felicity Pierce."

"Better she end things before the marriage ceremony if the man isn't the right one."

Cordie did smile at that. After all, she'd jilted a fiancé of her own before marrying Clayworth. "My thoughts exactly. So I told Brendan to invite the girl. I do hope you and Russ will make her feel welcome. She won't know a soul once she arrives."

And Cordie thought thrusting an unsuspecting, innocent girl in Russ' path was the best course to take? If Miss Pritchard was homely, it would probably be all right. Probably. "I'm sure we'll cross paths," he said, noncommittally.

"Meaning you don't intend to be around and you think that answer will dissuade me?"

She did know him better than most. "I'm not feeling all that social these days, Cor."

"So you're just going to hole up inside Avery House?"

And hope that he could somehow clear his mind of all thoughts of Phoebe Greywood in the process. "For the time being."

"I won't pretend to know all you've been through these last years, Tris." Cordie reached over and squeezed his hand. "But just don't become a hermit. Greg's already half-way there and I hate to lose both of you."

Oh, dear God. Tristan didn't want his future to look like his oldest brother's. Until now he'd never thought of himself as being remotely similar to Greg. However, Gregory Avery *had* lusted for a woman who belonged to another man, hadn't he? Perhaps they were more similar than Tristan had ever suspected, and that thought struck fear in his heart.

~~~

Up until the traveling coach lurched forward, taking Phoebe and her parents from their home on Curzon Street, she'd still held out hope that Captain Avery would make his appearance. However, that hope dissipated as she watched Mayfair pass outside the carriage window as though it had never existed. Things would be easier if something made sense. But nothing did. Had she done something to drive him away? If so, she had no idea what it could have been. She hadn't seen him long enough to do anything on that grand a scale.

Her mother caught her gaze across the coach and smiled, though it didn't reach her eyes. "Are you feeling all right, darling?"

Hardly. She felt as though her heart had been ripped from her chest. She felt lost. She felt as though everything she'd ever known in her life had ceased to make sense.

"I should stay here," Matthew grumbled.

"We have discussed this, Matthew," their father stated, his tone firm and unbending, like it always was.

"Well, someone ought to stay behind to hand Russell Avery his arse on a platter."

Mama gasped at the same time Papa's back stiffened. "That is all I want to hear out of you today, young man." When Matthew opened his mouth to respond, Papa growled, "One more word and you can ride up top with the coachman, Matthew."

Matthew deflated and sank against the squabs, refusing to meet their father's eye. Phoebe's own gaze drifted to the floor. Everyone in the coach was thinking the same thing. Everyone knew that her intended wanted nothing to do with her, but none of them said the words aloud. And that truth, that knowledge, broke what was left of her heart.

"Military men are different," Mama finally said, her voice much softer than normal. She shifted in her seat and touched Papa's chest. "Your own brother, Max. Simon left his motherless children to purse his glory. Tell her not to fret."

Slowly, Phoebe raised her gaze to meet her father's. Papa's blue eyes, so much like hers, seemed to assess her as though he was searching for something. "Your mother is right, sweetheart. It takes a certain kind of man to be a success on the battlefield, and by all accounts, Captain Avery was quite successful. What you will need to decide is if you can live with that sort of man. I don't imagine he's the sort who is moved by tears or women's sensibilities."

And yet he'd been the most charming man she'd ever met, up until this final campaign. He'd once hung on her every word. Kissed her softly. Appeared to love her with his entire heart.

Her father was correct, however. If this new man was who Russell now was, she still had a choice. Vows had yet to be spoken. She could always cry off. That idea twisted the shards of her heart. Cry off. Something she would have never considered as far back as a week ago. Of course, a week ago, she'd been fairly certain she possessed a fiancé who cared something for her.

"Don't be hasty," Mama added. "We'll invite him to Malvern Hall, and we shall see what sort of young man he is then, after he's settled back into English life."

Phoebe nodded in agreement, though she knew in the pit of her stomach that Russell would not travel to Norfolk to see her. After all, he hadn't had the inclination or found the time to travel but a few streets to do so for nearly a sennight.

Eight

SOME days Tristan wasn't certain if only a day had transpired or several years since he'd last seen Phoebe. Nights passed in one gaming hell or another. Days both flew by and then crawled to a standstill, but she was never far from his mind.

Somewhere along the way, Philip had returned to England. Cordie had worked her magic and helped the wounded and broken-hearted major fall for Miss Pritchard, though Tristan had no idea how his sister had managed that feat. But when the girl's jilted fiancé had actually gunned Philip down in retaliation, Tristan had jumped into the fray with both feet. He'd scoured London for the villain, hired guards and Bow Street Runners alike, relieved to have had something other than his tortured thoughts of Phoebe to focus his attention on. But once Philip and his new bride were safe and happily ensconced in Leverton Park, Tristan discovered the ache in his heart had only grown.

What he'd initially suspected was some sort of bizarre infatuation was, apparently, much more than that. But how such a thing had happened to him, he had no idea. A little voice in the back of his head whispered that he'd always loved her, but that was utter foolishness. Each time that thought crept into his mind, he pushed it away as quickly as he could.

"I knew Amelia was perfect for him," Russell said in way of greeting as he strode into the breakfast room.

Tristan glanced up from his untouched plate, his eyes landing on his brother. Though they lived in the same home, he and Russell might as well have lived in two different worlds. "I beg your pardon?"

"Amelia. She's cajoled him into being social, if you can believe it." Russell waived a folded piece of foolscap in the air. "A house party. A celebration in honor of our dear friend's marriage."

"Philip?" Tristan scratched his head. "Philip *Moore* is hosting a house party?" If Amelia Moore, nee Pritchard, had managed to pull off such a feat, it was nothing short of a miracle.

Russell agreed with a nod of his head. "I imagine half of the 45th will be there. He's asked if we wouldn't mind staying at Rufford Hall as he suspects the Park will be overrun with guests."

Their family seat. Tristan had yet to travel as far north as Nottinghamshire since his return from the continent. Perhaps the journey would be good for him. Once at Rufford Hall, perhaps he should remain there instead of returning to London with Russ. After all, Tristan could barely be in the same room with his brother these days. He couldn't stomach the awful sense of dread that washed over him after even the tiniest amount of time spent in his brother's company. He couldn't take hearing about Russell's unending list of conquests. He couldn't look at his brother knowing that someday — most likely sooner rather than later — Russell would marry Phoebe Greywood. Why hadn't he thought of returning home before now? Probably because Greg was an utter bore. But Greg's company had to be better than Russell's. "I'm sure Mother would be annoyed if we stayed anywhere else."

"There is that," Russell agreed. Then he dropped into a seat across from Tristan and gestured for a footman to pour him a cup of coffee. "You'll never guess who I saw last night."

"Oh?" Tristan asked warily as scooped his baked eggs onto his toast.

"The new Viscount Brookfield."

Tristan dropped his fork on his plate. "Brookfield?" He studied his brother in surprise, as the late Viscount Brookfield had nearly killed their brother-in-law the previous year. "What the devil is Andrew Yeats doing here?"

Russell took a sip of his coffee, then shrugged. "I can't speak for the present, but last night he was enjoying a pair of girls. Russian twins, to be precise."

Of course he was. It wouldn't have even been possible for Russ to have bumped into Andrew Yeats some place respectable. "Did you speak with him?" The man was more than a little dangerous.

"Busy myself at the time." Russell shook his head. "Doubt he recognized me. It's been a million years since

Eton."

Tristan would remember Andrew Yeats no matter how long it had been. They were the same age and had shared many of the same lessons over the years. It would be good to know if the man held any ill will toward Cordie and Clayworth for his uncle's untimely death.

"Must have sorted out that financial predicament the late Brookfield landed the viscountcy in."

Tristan's brow rose in silent question.

"Well," his brother explained, "those pretty Russians could cost a man an arm and a leg. He didn't appear destitute."

Ah. That explained it. Russell probably knew down to the farthing how much those pretty Russians would cost a man. Distracted from his thoughts on Brookfield, Tristan frowned at his brother. "Aren't you tired of the life you're leading?"

Russell simply frowned at him and said, "Tired?" as though the word was a foreign one he'd never heard before.

Tristan snorted. Why had he bothered to ask? Russ would never tire of his whoring, not until he was on his deathbed. Maybe not even then. "You *do* have a fiancée, you might remember. I wouldn't be surprised if news of your exploits have made it all the way to Norfolk. You should keep that in mind as you're making your swath across Town."

At that comment, Russell smirked. "Who would have thought *you* would champion Phoebe?"

How Tristan itched to pummel that smirk off his brother's face. He balled his hand into a fist and ground out, "Regardless of my opinions about the lady, *you* offered for her. She accepted, and she deserves better treatment than you've shown her thus far."

That blasted smirk only grew wider. "If I didn't know better, I'd think you were Philip Moore with your lack of humor."

"Humor?" Tristan echoed. "What is humorous about the way you've treated the girl you're to marry? Do show me the humor in it, Russ, because I am missing it."

His brother heaved a beleaguered sigh. "It's humorous to find you, of all people, carrying her banner. Besides," he shook his head, "I'm not married to her yet."

"And when you are, you'll suddenly be a knight errant?"

"When did you become so boring, Tris?" Russell took another swallow of his coffee.

Boring. Tristan glared at his brother. "Why did you even ask her to marry you?"

"Not this again," Russell grumbled. "I know you don't like the chit, but what's done is done and there's no going back, no matter how much I might want to. I said I'd marry her and I will."

Oh, he was so magnanimous. He made it sound as though taking Phoebe Greywood to husband would be a hardship, as though he was doing her a favor. But that was the furthest thing from the truth. Russell was cursing the poor girl, not favoring her. "Then show her the respect she deserves. She's stuck with you forever and a day. Respect is the least she's owed, Russ."

His brother snorted in response, which only inflamed Tristan's ire.

Tristan pushed his chair away from the breakfast table. "If you don't treat Miss Greywood like the lady she is, I swear on Father's grave I'll kill you with my bare hands." No longer able to stomach Russell's company, Tristan strode from the breakfast room without so much as a glance back at his older brother.

If Russell loved or cared about Phoebe, Tristan could more easily accept his fate - namely, that she would never be his. But that wasn't the case. Russell only cared about himself and the pleasure of any given moment. How could Tristan stand by the rest of his life and bear witness as Phoebe's unhappiness played out before him? How could he watch her heart break time and again by Russell's careless deeds? She deserved so much better. But those thoughts never brought him any solace.

"Tris!" Russell called after him, though Tristan refused to acknowledge his brother.

Damn it all. What was he going to do? How was he to get out of this entangled mess? Because unless Tristan wanted to find himself living out of a bottle the rest of his days, he was going to have to sort something out, or perhaps leave England all together. And sooner rather than later for his own sanity.

He suddenly missed life on the continent where strategy and battle plans took precedence over matters of the heart. But the war was over, and his services were no longer needed in that regard. Still, there were other regiments in other places, weren't there?

India.

Canada.

The Caribbean.

Somewhere, anywhere other than here.

Nine

THERE was nothing in the world quite as delightful as the slightly salty Norfolk air against Phoebe's face as she raced along the shoreline. And nothing quite as relaxing as the sound of the waves crashing onto the beach. Home was so much more peaceful than Town life. Home was perfect.

"Phoebe!" came Felicity's voice on the wind.

Phoebe pulled back on the mare's reins and looked over her shoulder to find her friend several lengths behind. "And you were so sure you were going to beat me, Lissy," she laughed.

A moment later Felicity drew up beside Phoebe, her blonde curls a tangled mess about her shoulders and her bonnet long since gone. "I had no idea you were such an apt horsewoman," her friend grumbled. "You can barely walk ten paces without your step faltering."

"Well, Hemera does all the walking for me." Phoebe

stroked her mare's neck, completely unperturbed by Felicity's jab. After all, it was hardly the first time she'd heard such a comment. Matthew had outdone himself over the years in that regard. "Besides, I've been riding longer than I've been walking."

"Then maybe you should *ride* Hemera into your next ball."

"Can you imagine the look on my mother's face if I suggested that?" Phoebe urged her mare forward and Felicity fell in beside her. "It might just be worth it."

"She only wants what's best for you."

"She wants to keep me in the dark," Phoebe countered. Then she tilted her head toward her friend. "I overheard my parents arguing last night."

"Overheard?"

Phoebe shrugged. Overheard, eavesdropped. No matter which way the hairs were split, the outcome was the same. "Papa has heard the same rumors we have from Town. My Uncle James sent a rather detailed report, apparently." And Phoebe had to believe all the awful things she'd heard about Russell were true. There were simply too many stories filtering into Malvern Hall for them to all be false. Besides, her uncle would never have sent the report he had if the tales were not based in fact.

When the first whispers had reached her ears a few months ago, she'd been hurt, then numb, but now… Well, she wasn't certain what she was now.

Felicity heaved a sigh. "Did your father want to return to London and string the captain up by his bollocks?"

"Lissy!" Phoebe's mouth dropped open at her

friend's choice of words, and she was relieved to have such an excellent seat or else she would have fallen right off Hemera.

An unrepentant grin flashed on Felicity's face. "Well, I would expect Luke to do so for me if I was in your position. In fact, I'd be rather put out with him if he didn't do so."

Though Phoebe's father hadn't suggested anything quite so colorful, he and Felicity were of like minds. "Mama wants to be patient. To wait until Captain Avery visits before we make any rash decisions."

"We?" Felicity echoed. "Is she marrying him too? I had no idea." Then she shook her head as they started up a gentle slope. "Don't listen to me, I know I'm jaded, but don't listen to your mother either. You need to make up your own mind. It is your future, after all. No one else has to live it but you."

She knew Phoebe was right. If only things made some sense, it would be easier to know what to do. "You remember how he used to be, don't you?"

Felicity nodded, but she said nothing, her lips pursed together.

"He did used to seem enamored with me, didn't he? I didn't imagine all of that, did I?" she wondered aloud, finally giving voice to the words she hadn't dared utter until now.

Pity flashed in Felicity's eyes. "You didn't imagine it. Luke says men are fickle. Dangle a pretty thing before them and you have their interest until another pretty thing comes along."

What a horrible thing to say! Phoebe's heart clinched at hearing those awful words. "Your brother-in-law said that to you? I hardly think your sister would appreciate the sentiment."

Felicity shook her head. "Luke says that's how he was until he met Juliet. That's why he's ever vigilant when it comes to my suitors, not that he needs to worry in my case."

So if a man met the right girl—or rather, if a man met his true love—he would be true to her? That theory didn't speak well for her situation with Russell, did it? Assuming Lucas Beckford's theory was correct—and who knew the mind of a rake better than a reformed one—then everything was very simple. Phoebe wasn't the girl for Russell.

As soon as the thought entered her mind, she knew it was correct. And if she wasn't the girl for Russell, then he couldn't be the man for her. After all, the man for her wouldn't treat her so callously, would he?

A coldness washed over Phoebe as her path suddenly became clear. Even so, the entire situation left her feeling slightly numb. "Let us discuss something else."

"Very well. Juliet has summoned me home," Felicity blurted out as they started back toward the treeline that would take them down the path, back to Malvern Hall.

Phoebe's head snapped up to look at Felicity, who had avoided her family seat as best as she could ever since her return from America. She was certain her mouth hung open. "Prestwick Chase?"

"You said you wanted to discuss something else." Felicity shrugged. "It seems my sister is expecting again and wishes for me to attend her."

"So you're going."

"I can't very well leave her care to Luke or Carraway now, can I?" Still, she sounded far from thrilled at the prospect of returning home, not that Phoebe could blame her. Prestwick Chase had been the scene of more than one unhappy event in Felicity's life.

"I'll miss you, but I'm sure Juliet will be glad to have you," Phoebe said measuredly.

"I'm sure the entire thing will be positively dreadful." A mirthless laugh escaped Felicity. "I'm not Georgie. I am not a good caretaker. I am happily spoiled and prefer to keep it that way."

Phoebe couldn't help the laugh that escaped her. Felicity was nothing if not honest. Still, despite her protestations, Felicity was a dear friend and her sister would be in good hands once she arrived in Derbyshire.

In the distance, Phoebe spotted Malvern Hall standing proudly against a rapidly darkening sky. They'd best get home before rain started to fall. Phoebe flashed a grin at her friend and said, "I'll race you back to the stables." Then she urged Hemera to a gallop and then to a run before Felicity's objections could reach her ears.

Phoebe leaned closer to her mare, loving the breeze whipping through her hair and the speed of the horse beneath her. Malvern Hall grew larger and larger until Phoebe reached her grandfather's stables and she reined Hemera to a stop.

She handed the reins to one of the grooms and then dismounted, only to have her feet slide out from under her before she landed on her bottom. "Ouch," she grumbled to herself.

"Miss Greywood!" The groom rushed around the

mare and offered her his hand. "Are you all right?"

Phoebe nodded hastily. She'd survive. After all, she'd certainly suffered worse spills in her days, as Tristan Avery loved to remind her. At least that brutish lieutenant wasn't present to laugh at her this time. Black-hearted boor.

Phoebe thanked the groom for his assistance and brushed the dirt from her riding habit just as Felicity barreled through the gates and thunder rumbled overhead.

"You are positively wild, Phoebe Greywood!" her friend declared. Of course Felicity dismounted her mare with the grace that came from being a duke's daughter, even if she was only half English. If it wasn't for her mass of untamed hair, Felicity would look regal enough to attend Prinny and his set at Carlton House.

"Indeed!" came Mama's voice, just a few feet away. "Do have a care, Phoebe."

Perfect. All Phoebe needed was a lecture on hoydenistic behaviors. She turned to face her mother and found her brandishing an invitation in the air and wearing a victorious smile.

"What's that, Mama?"

"Wonderful news, but let's get inside before the rain begins." Her mother gestured towards the manor. "I cannot believe you girls thought to ride with grey skies overhead."

"There's always grey skies overhead," Felicity muttered under her breath, but Phoebe was more curious about her mother's correspondence than she was her friend's remark.

"Do tell me what's arrived," Phoebe urged as she

linked her arm with Felicity's.

"Oh, darling," Mama gushed as the trio started on the path that lead to the manor house. "We have been invited to Rufford Hall! Isn't that perfect?"

Rufford Hall? The family seat of the Averys?

Perfect wasn't the word that sprang to Phoebe's mind. In fact, queasiness washed over her. "Captain Avery invited us to Rufford Hall?" That made no sense at all. Why would he send for her now after all of the carousing he'd done all summer? After rejecting Papa's repeated offers to visit Malvern Hall?

"No, no, no," Mama rushed to explain. "*Lord* Avery has invited us." Then she beamed like the happiest schoolgirl despite the droplet of rain that plopped onto her nose. "Oh, darling, now everything will turn out all right. You'll see."

Phoebe was fairly certain that her idea of all right and her mother's were vastly different in this case. Russell hadn't sent for her at all, his oldest brother had. Phoebe exchanged a glance with Felicity who looked just as doubtful that everything would turn out all right as Phoebe felt.

"Lord Avery?" Phoebe echoed.

There was only one reason why the reclusive and self-absorbed Lord Avery would invite the Greywoods to Rufford Hall. His meddlesome sister, Cordie Clayworth, must have had her hands full to pull off such a feat.

"Yes, yes," Mama continued. "It seems Major Moore and his new wife are hosting an event at Leverton Park and Lord Avery would like us all to be his and the captain's guests for the festivities."

Heavens! Phoebe's mouth went dry. The last place on Earth she wanted to be was Rufford Hall. Not with the less than friendly Lord Avery, not with Russell's villainous mother, and most certainly not with that brutish Tristan Avery. It was hard enough to abide him in small doses. She couldn't imagine sleeping under the same roof as the man.

"Once Captain Avery sees you again, all will be right with the world," Mama promised.

But nothing could be further from the truth. Phoebe wasn't the girl for Russell Avery and he wasn't the man for her. Still, she didn't figure she had much of a choice about whether or not to visit Rufford Hall. Her mother would have her way in that. At least, Phoebe supposed, it would give her the chance to end her betrothal face to face. Not that Russell had earned such consideration. Even still, it seemed the decent thing to do. While Russell Avery might not be decent himself, Phoebe most assuredly was.

Ten

THANK God for Leverton Park and the respite it offered from Rufford Hall. "Please tell me there's room at the inn," Tristan begged his old friend, Major Philip Moore, as he sank into a chair across from the man's desk.

The major eyed Tristan as though he was a specimen Philip had never seen before. "Room at the inn?" he echoed. "Is there an expectant virgin needing shelter that I'm unaware of?"

Tristan ignored his friend's sarcasm. "I'll even sleep in your stables, if there's room. Just don't make me return to Rufford Hall tonight."

At that Philip tipped his head back and laughed. "Is Lady Avery showering you in attention? So relieved her baby boy has returned home from the war in one piece?"

She was doing a bit of that, though hovering was probably a better word for his mother's actions. Tristan nodded his head. "And Gregory is surlier than I remember. And Russell is… Russell." Besides, the Greywoods were to arrive today, and Tristan thought it best he keep his distance from Phoebe and her family. After all, no good could come of him spending time in close proximity to the girl. Had he known she'd been invited to the Hall, Tristan would never have left London in the first place. Blast Cordie and her interfering ways.

"It can't be all that bad, Tris." Philip leaned back in his chair as though to study Tristan from a different angle. "You're fortunate you're surrounded by family who cares about you."

Tristan shrugged, as he didn't feel fortunate about much these days. "With the exception of Cordie," he corrected. "So either let me stay in your stables or toss my sister from Leverton Park. She's the only sibling whose company I actually enjoy anymore."

Philip snorted. "Amelia would have my head. She's never hosted anything like this before, and Cordie's the only familiar face in the sea of people who've invaded our halls."

"You did invite them," Tristan grumbled. "They didn't all show up of their own accord, you know."

"You are welcome to spend as much time here as you like, my friend. But I don't have any free chambers to spare."

Which Tristan had known. The Park was nearly overflowing with past and current regiment members and their families. Still, it hadn't hurt to ask. "I suppose I could always turn tail and retreat back to London."

"London, hmm?" Philip eyed him with concern. "As luck would have it, I received an interesting missive from London this morning."

"Did you?" Tristan asked.

"Mmm. Lord Bathurst, to be precise." Philip's serious, dark eyes bored into Tristan.

Who knew the War Office would act so quickly? "And how is his lordship?"

"Don't play coy. Why in the world do you want to join the 16th in Canada? You were just as anxious to return home as I was."

He had been all those months ago. Very anxious to return to England. To never leave her shores again. But all of that had changed. "Discovered I prefer to live abroad. What did you tell him?"

"I've written that your bravery is unparalleled and you'd be an asset to any commander lucky enough to have you."

"Thank you," Tristan sighed. He'd been afraid his old friend would try to talk him from his current course.

"I haven't sent it yet, Tris." Philip leaned back in his chair, his countenance darker than it had been in a while. "I also haven't been besieged by Cordie yet, begging me to talk sense into you. So I'm assuming you haven't shared these plans with your family."

Philip did know him very well, and Cordie for that matter. "It's not their choice. Cordie has her own family she should worry about. Greg and I have never seen eye to eye on much. And…" Tristan's gaze drifted to the rug at his feet. "And Russ will marry Miss Greywood sooner rather than later. There's not really a place for me here, Philip. But I know how to be an officer, how to take and give orders."

Philip heaved a sigh. "I owe you my life."

"And I owe you mine." Something Tristan could never repay. Finally, he met his friend's gaze once more.

Philip shook his head. "But I owe you Amelia's life too. So if you want me to send that letter, I will. I just wish you'd give it more thought, Tris."

Tristan had thought of very little else since the idea had come to him. At least this way he wouldn't have to witness the disaster that was sure to be his brother's marriage. At least this way he could focus on something other than Phoebe Greywood. At least this way he might find some peace. "Send the letter, Philip. I'll be in your debt."

"I wouldn't tell those men out there—" the major gestured toward the corridor with his head "—that you're joining the 16th. They'll probably feel betrayed."

That was a good point. "I shall wait until your house party is over to tell anyone else."

A knock came at the study door, then it opened and Amelia Moore stepped into the room, her arms folded across her middle. "An entire house full of soldiers and the two of you are hiding in here?"

As Tristan stood to greet the lady, Philip reached for his cane and used it to push to his feet. "We just had a bit of business, my love." The major limped toward his wife. "We'll come out of hiding, now."

Tristan smiled at the pair. He'd never thought to see Philip happy again after everything he'd been through. Tristan would adore Amelia Moore all of her days for restoring his friend to the man he'd once been, in spirit if not in stature. "A house full of soldiers?" he echoed her earlier words. "And what of countesses? I have yet to lay eyes on my sister."

Amelia winced a bit. "She's not feeling well at the moment, Tristan. I just sent her to lie down."

"She's not feeling well?"

"She vows she'll be back on her feet by dinner."

Philip chuckled. "Then she will be. I've never known Cordie to fail at anything she put her mind to."

"She did ask," Amelia began, "for me to make certain Miss Greywood would visit tomorrow, however. Will you pass on that invitation when you return to Rufford Hall?"

Tristan nodded, as it was clearly expected. "As soon as I arrive home, Amelia. And do tell her I hope she feels better in the morning."

※

"Oh, Miss Greywood!" Lady Avery gushed as she pulled Phoebe into her embrace. "We are so glad you have finally arrived!"

It took every bit of self-control Phoebe had not to recoil from the woman. Others among the *ton* might believe the baroness to be the gregarious lady she pretended to be, but Phoebe knew exactly what sort of monster Lady Avery was. One benefit to ending her betrothal to Russell would be that this woman would never be her mother-in-law. But for now, she had to play the part of the anxious fiancée, at least until the end of this farce of a visit, or the next fortnight would be unbearable.

"It's so nice to see you, my lady," Phoebe lied.

Lady Avery released her and then turned her attention to Phoebe's parents. "Evelyn, how do you always look so lovely even after traveling?"

"You're too kind, Gladys," Mama replied.

"And, Mr. Greywood, we are so pleased you were all able to make the trip. Come, come!" The baroness gestured toward the closest parlor. "Let us adjourn in here so we can all reacquaint ourselves." She glanced at the aged butler, standing by the door. "Browne, inform my sons that our guests have arrived and then have some refreshments delivered as well."

"Yes, milady."

Phoebe gulped. For the last sennight she'd dreaded this event, of the moment she would finally see Russell again. She followed the baroness into the parlor and quickly claimed a yellow chintz chair so that she wouldn't have to sit beside Lady Avery or any of her less than desirable sons. Mama frowned a bit at her as she assumed a spot on a settee next to the baroness, who clasped Mama's hands in hers as though they were the closest of friends.

Matthew and Papa found their own spots just as Captain Avery stepped over the threshold, tall and handsome as ever in his regimentals. Phoebe sucked in a breath as her fiancé's green eyes sought her gaze. Then Russell Avery smiled, reminding her at once of the charming man she'd been so infatuated with all those many months ago.

"Phoebe," Russell breathed out, as though he was truly happy to see her. Then he crossed the floor to her chair and reached out his hand. Phoebe placed her hand in his and she couldn't help her heart from lifting a bit when he bowed before her and touched his lips to her knuckles. "It has been too long."

Too long, indeed. All of the sordid tales that had reached her over the last several months rang once more in her ears. She couldn't let him charm her with his handsome smile and his courtly manners, not now that she knew him to be so perfidious in nature. "Yes, Captain, it has been too long."

⁂

Dread washed over Tristan as he drew his horse to a halt in his brother's stable yard. A coach with the Malvern crest rested not far away, and he knew that every bit of peace he'd enjoyed at Rufford Hall, though it had been found few and far between, had come to an end.

He dismounted his hunter and handed his reins to an awaiting footman before turning his attention to the Tudor manor where he'd spent his youth. Perhaps it would be better than he thought. Perhaps when he laid eyes on Phoebe, he would find that she wasn't the lovely creature he imagined her to be each night as he drifted to sleep and each morning as he woke. Perhaps seeing her again would wake him from the terrible spell he'd been under since he last saw her. Perhaps. Anything was possible, after all.

He started for the garden door, but stopped when a familiar giggle hit his ears. Phoebe. He'd know that tinkling sound anywhere and despite his mind urging him to flee, his feet followed the sound down a path toward the garden. Tristan rounded a hedge and... the air whooshed out of him.

His heart ached at the sight of her, just as beautiful as he remembered, leaning on Russell's arm and beaming up at him as though he'd hung the moon and each star in the sky. Her auburn hair was piled high on her head and pretty ringlets framed her face. A muscle twitched beside Tristan's eye. Seeing her was even worse than he'd imagined, especially having to witness her batting her lashes at his unworthy brother.

"Tristan!" Russell waved him toward the pair. "Come say hello to my darling Phoebe."

Tristan managed not to snort. *My darling Phoebe.* Russell was certainly putting on quite the performance, wasn't he? Tristan must have finally succeeded in striking the fear of God in his brother after the last time they spoke on the subject of his betrothed. At least Tristan could say he had done that for Phoebe then — made certain Russell treated her with the respect she was due.

He navigated the path around a couple of his mother's topiaries until he stood before his brother and Phoebe. Dear God, surviving the next fortnight would be the death of him. "Miss Greywood," he said, and tried to ignore the pain in his heart as her blue eyes, which reminded him in that instant of an Italian summer sky, met his.

Eleven

PHOEBE blinked at Lieutenant Avery. Certainly she hadn't done anything that would warrant the frown displayed so prominently on his face. He looked positively tortured. Of course, just her presence always seemed to put him in a temper. Wouldn't he be thrilled when she cried off and he wouldn't have to worry about coming face to face with her at family gatherings any longer? "Lieutenant," she murmured.

"I, um—" he cleared his throat "—just left Leverton Park, and Mrs. Moore asked about you, Miss Greywood."

"About me?" Phoebe touched a hand to her heart. She'd never even met Mrs. Moore. Strange the lady should ask about her. He'd probably said something horrid that piqued the lady's interest.

Tristan Avery cleared his throat once more, which must be the result of a guilty conscience. "Cordie apparently mentioned you. So Mrs. Moore asked me to invite you to Leverton Park tomorrow."

"Oh." Cordie had mentioned her? Of course she did. Her friend was still under the delusion that they would be sisters soon. All things considered, she would like to see Cordie again. Besides, visiting Leverton Park had to be better than remaining at Rufford Hall. "Well, I look forward to meeting her then."

Russell groaned. "Oh, I am sorry, my darling. But I have something that requires my attention tomorrow."

Did he? Some tavern wench in the nearby village, perhaps? Phoebe forced herself to smile at the lying blackguard. "Oh, well, I wouldn't feel right going without you, Captain." Let him weasel his way out of that.

"I'm sure Tristan wouldn't mind escorting you." Russell's gaze flashed to his brother. "You don't mind, do you? I know how much regard you hold for Miss Greywood, and we do want to make sure she is well entertained while she's here."

The muscle twitching near the lieutenant's right eye and his clenched jaw spoke volumes about his regard for her. Phoebe managed not to roll her eyes.

"I doubt the lady can keep up with my hunter. Perhaps you can escort her after you've dealt with whatever it is that requires *your* attention."

Clearly, neither of them wanted to spend time with her. Well, she didn't want to spend time with them either. Still, she wouldn't allow the brute to insult her equestrian skills. "The lieutenant is correct. Rufford Hall is hardly known for its horseflesh. I can't imagine you have anything fast enough to suit me."

Tristan Avery scoffed. "Only a Bedlamite would put *you* on horseback."

"I beg your pardon?" Phoebe's back straightened and she looked the boorish man directly in his supercilious green eyes.

"Rufford Hall may not be known for its horseflesh, Miss Greywood. But you are hardly known for your surefootedness. I won't have you take a fall and be forced to carry your lifeless body back to your parents."

Oh, that was the outside of enough. Odious, reprehensible man! Phoebe squared her shoulders. "If I arrive at Leverton Park without incident, I want you to promise never to mock my surefootedness ever again, Lieutenant."

He raised one half-amused eyebrow. "And if you fall, Miss Greywood?"

Blast the arrogant man! "What if I beat you?"

"Do you know the way?" he asked, the smug brute.

Well, he had her there. Curse him. "No," she admitted through gritted teeth.

"Then I can't imagine how you could possibly beat me."

Oh, she would love to see him fall. She would pay every penny she owned to bear witness to his downfall.

"Well," Russell Avery began before Phoebe could think of something fitting to retort, "it sounds like the two of you will have a wonderful time sorting all of that out. I can't wait to hear all about it." Then a smile broke across his face. "Just do remember that Miss Greywood is our guest and should be treated with the utmost *respect*, Tristan."

The look Lieutenant Avery flashed his brother would

have halted the whole of Caesar's invading army had he been in the British Isles at the time. A pity he hadn't been with those ancient Celts, because had he been then he wouldn't be here now.

Tristan was in hell. Or purgatory. Or wherever it was that souls went to suffer for all time and eternity. Stuck between his mother on one side and Mrs. Greywood on the other, he sat across the dinner table from Phoebe, which gave him a front row view of the object of his affection. He'd had to watch every smile she cast his brother, every bat of her lashes, hear every giggle Russell elicited from her. And between the bookends of their mothers, he couldn't leave, grumble or even heave a frustrated sigh.

Phoebe seemed oblivious to his torture, but then her eyes locked with his and Tristan's breath caught in his throat. Damn it all. He could gaze at her the rest of his life and never tire of seeing her. What harm was there is gazing upon her? He really should let his eyes drink their fill. After all, when he left for Canada, he'd never see her again. The images he saved now might be all to keep him warm in the days and years to come.

She frowned slightly at him as though she couldn't fathom why he was looking at her. Of course, if she had any inkling of his thoughts, she'd probably run straight back to London as fast as her feet would carry her, stumbling all the way. Even still, Tristan couldn't drag his eyes from her. Russell was the luckiest bastard on Earth, damn him. He had everything Tristan could ever hope for, but he didn't appreciate his lot at all.

Phoebe's azure eyes narrowed on Tristan. Chagrined,

he smiled, which only made her eyes narrow even more. They couldn't go on like this, she'd be squinting before long. So Tristan looked away, muttered something to his mother about her choice for the evening's menu, and then turned his attention to his plate.

It seemed like an eternity before the ladies retired to the drawing room, leaving the men to their port. Thirteen more nights like this one. Tristan wasn't certain he'd make it.

"It's so kind of you to escort Phoebe to Leverton Park tomorrow." Matthew Greywood assumed the spot beside Tristan. "Offering her an olive branch, are you?"

Tristan shrugged. "She'll be my sister soon enough."

The young man glanced down the table in Russell's direction. "Not if it was up to me."

"I beg your pardon?" Tristan turned his full attention on the man.

Matthew Greywood shook his head. "I'll be the first fellow to say that Phoebe can exasperate me better than anyone else, but she *is* my sister. And she deserves better than your brother."

And while Tristan agreed whole-heartedly, he couldn't really say as much to the Greywood heir. "Unless you'd like Russell to put a ball in your chest, you'd better watch your tongue."

The young man snorted. "I'm not afraid of him."

"Then you're a fool," Tristan replied. "I've seen him take down men larger than you and come away completely unscathed."

"Perhaps," Matthew Greywood began. "But I'd wager none of them were defending their sister's honor."

Tristan shook his head. "No. They were defending their own lives."

Greywood winced, but then he lifted his chin stubbornly. "It's my duty to defend my sister."

"You'd spend your time more wisely trying to get her to cry off, rather than forcing nobility on him." Tristan lifted his port to his mouth and took a hefty swallow.

"Can't you talk to him?" Matthew Greywood pressed quietly.

Tristan cast the man a sidelong glance. "I'm not my brother's keeper, nor does he pay my council any attention."

"Which is as much attention as Phoebe pays mine."

"Then I supposed they're both doomed, aren't they?"

"What does one do when one sees a carriage accident before it happens?" The man gazed into his own glass of port, though he'd yet to indulge.

"Hope the passengers are thrown to safety."

Matthew Greywood's frown deepened. "I don't see how that's possible."

"Neither do I," Tristan agreed, though he wished he did. He wished he saw a way out of the situation for Phoebe, but if she wouldn't listen to reason, which she didn't seem likely to do; if she didn't realize the predicament she was in; if she didn't suddenly come to her senses, she'd be doomed to a miserable existence with Russell the rest of her days.

Twelve

PHOEBE cinched her wrapper tightly around her waist then slipped from her chambers into the corridor. The tapers on the walls lit her way as she padded along the hallway and down the stairs, making her way toward the library. A boring treatise of one sort or another would help keep her mind from spinning and allow her to finally drift off to sleep. Every time she closed her eyes, she saw Russell's smiling face, which was more than a little unsettling. He almost reminded her of the man he'd been before he left for that last campaign. But he wasn't that man, and she doubted he ever had been.

A creak sounded under her foot and Phoebe stopped in her tracks. The last thing she wanted was to alert anyone to her presence. Heaven forbid she come across Russell or worse – Lady Avery – in the dead of night. Perfect. Now she'd most likely have nightmares. Images of Cordie's bruised and scarred body would flash in her mind all night. A shiver ran down her spine at the memory of the injuries her friend had suffered at the hands of own mother.

Phoebe glanced around the corridor. No one seemed to have heard her, so she lifted the hem of her wrapper and nightrail and hastened her pace toward the library. A warm glow emanated from inside the room in question, and she hurried toward it as though salvation waited just inside.

As soon as she crossed the threshold into the library, a familiar voice said, "Looking for something on Ancient Rome?"

Phoebe gasped and her step faltered, but she caught her balance before she tumbled to the ground.

Tristan Avery lounged across a settee near the middle of the room, his boots resting on the arm, his eyes trained on her.

Thank heavens she hadn't fallen! The last thing she needed was to make a fool of herself in front of him again. "What are you doing here?" she demanded.

"I live here," he replied, not bothering at all to stand like a gentleman would. Then he lifted a tumbler of some amber drink in the air towards her in a mock toast. "The better question is what are you doing here?"

He had certainly been odd tonight, hadn't he? Staring at her all through dinner, and then *smiling*. He was up to something. Not that it mattered. He could plot away to his heart's content. When she left Rufford Hall in a fortnight, she'd never have to lay eyes on the brutish lieutenant ever again. "Just looking for something that will put me to sleep."

He raised his glass toward her again. "Whisky will work better than anything Greg has in here to read."

Whisky? Phoebe's mouth dropped open. She was not about to drink whisky, and certainly not with him. "I think not, thank you."

A wry smile lit his lips. "Suit yourself."

As though she would do something like that. Phoebe tipped her head back regally and stepped toward one of the far bookcases, hoping to put as much distance between herself and the lieutenant as possible.

"Chaucer is right there to your left."

Phoebe closed her eyes and gritted her teeth. "I can find something on my own."

"Just trying to be of service."

Oh, he'd always been so helpful, hadn't he? Always the perfect gentleman.

Phoebe snorted. "I don't need your service." Still, she couldn't help her eyes straying to a dark brown spine to her left with *Chaucer Works* emblazoned in gold. Blast him. She did love *The Canterbury Tales*. She reached for the book and then scowled when he chuckled from his spot on the settee.

"You're welcome."

She had the urge to hurl the book at his head, but instead she tilted her neck so he could better see her scowl.

"Oh come now," he urged, sitting a little taller on the settee. "You're too beautiful to ruin it with such a look."

Phoebe shook her head. "You think you're so charming, don't you?"

The lieutenant's smile faded away. "Not nearly charming enough." He slid his feet from the settee and sat up tall. "Come, sit."

Why? Did he have a dagger he was ready to plunge into her heart? Her face must have said as much because he laughed once more.

"So suspicious, Miss Greywood." He patted the place beside him. "If we're to be family soon, shouldn't we find some way to get along?"

As they weren't going to be family at all, there was no reason for them to get along or to ever have any sort of interaction after this dratted house party ended. But it was still too soon to say as much to Tristan or to Russell. "There are many families that don't get along at all," she said instead, as she crossed the floor toward him anyway.

Lieutenant Avery smiled up at her. "Not to fear, my dear, you won't have to abide me much longer."

No, she didn't. But how did he know that? "Oh?" she asked tartly. "Are you headed off on some wild adventure, never to return home?"

"Indeed." He nodded. "I just haven't told anyone yet."

That was certainly the last thing she expected him to say. Phoebe blinked at him. Had he coshed her over the head with a brick, she'd have been less surprised. "I beg your pardon?" She dropped onto the settee beside him. "What do you mean by that?"

"Just what you said. I'll soon be headed off on a wild adventure, never to return home."

He had to be kidding. He'd just returned home. By all accounts, he loved being home. "Where are you headed?"

"Canada," he replied evenly, though his green eyes seemed to linger on her features as though he was searching for something.

"Canada?"

"I don't know if that qualifies for wild adventure, but I'll do my best to ensure that it does."

Phoebe slid closer to him on the settee. Cordie would

be heartbroken if her favorite brother left England for good. "Why are you going to Canada?"

He heaved a sigh, then a self-deprecating smile settled on his face. "Once Waterloo was over, I couldn't wait to return home. I never thought I'd leave English shores again, but home—" his eyes seemed to study her once more "—wasn't what I anticipated, and I've come to realize it'll be best if I make my way in the world elsewhere."

There was something he wasn't saying, something important, if his expression was any indication. "Why? What did you anticipate?"

"I didn't anticipate falling in love," he said matter-of-factly.

That didn't make any sense at all. "And you think the best way to deal with the situation is to flee the country?" She couldn't help the laugh that escaped her. "Most men would court the girl, Lieutenant."

"True." He agreed with a nod. "But in my case, the girl belongs to another fellow. I don't think I can stay here, only to watch her spend her life with him. No, it'll be best for me to make my own way in Canada."

That was awful. And though Phoebe had never cared for Lieutenant Avery, her heart couldn't help but ache for him. A broken heart she understood. "I am sorry."

"Not nearly as sorry as I am." He flashed her a smile once more. "So, in the time I have left, Miss Greywood, why don't we make an effort to get along? It won't be too long, after all, before I cross the Atlantic and you won't have to see me again."

"Cordie doesn't know?"

"You're the only one I've told." He leaned toward

her, his green eyes seeking…something. "Can I trust you to keep my secret?"

She didn't like the idea of keeping things from Cordie. She was one of Phoebe's dearest friends, after all; but the sincerity she saw reflected in his eyes, made her heart constrict. The poor man. "I won't tell a soul," she promised.

~~~

Tristan had never seen a sight as beautiful as Phoebe, her unbound dark tresses trailing over her slender shoulders, her silk wrapper lying lovingly against her curves, her azure eyes focused so intently on him. For a brief moment it was easy to imagine leaning forward, cupping her face with his hands and pressing his lips to hers. Such imaginings would keep him warm in the years to come. "Thank you," he finally said, settling back on the settee to let his eyes drink their fill of her.

"But do you have to leave? Is there no other answer? Sometimes the future we've imagined for ourselves is simply not to be, through no fault of our own. Perhaps if you met another girl…"

How very surreal to be having this conversation with *her*. Tristan shook his head. "I'm afraid that's not possible. I've tried for months to get her off my mind, to no avail. If I could choose not to love her, I would, Miss Greywood. Alas, my feelings for her have only grown in strength. Leaving for parts unknown is my only option."

"Have you told her?" She captured his hand in hers and desire washed over him at the contact. "Have you told your paragon how you feel? Perhaps she feels the same and…"

Tristan could go on touching her the rest of his life,

but that was not to be. "I'm afraid she doesn't care for me. In fact, she finds my company reprehensible most of the time."

"I know how she feels," she muttered. Then an impish grin settled on her face. "I mean you *can* have that affect on ladies."

No. Just her. Still, Tristan shrugged. "I'll have to take your word for that."

She squeezed his hand and heaved a sigh. "Good luck to you, Lieutenant. In Canada, I mean." Then she slid her hand from his and rose from her spot. "And thank you for the Chaucer."

"Of course," he murmured, hating that their moment had, apparently, come to an end. "Do get your sleep, Miss Greywood. You'll want to be your most rested tomorrow at Leverton Park."

"And you get yours, sir. You'll need it if you're to best me on horseback."

He couldn't help the laugh that escaped him. "We'll take the Avery coach, just to be safe."

"You don't think I can ride," she said petulantly.

He certainly wouldn't take that chance. "I haven't seen any evidence to suggest that you can."

"You are a boor."

He agreed with an incline of his head. "Exactly what my love has told me, so it must be true. But we're still taking the coach."

Thirteen

PHOEBE had assumed when Lieutenant Avery had decreed they would be taking the coach to Leverton Park that he meant *they* would be taking the coach to Leverton Park, not that she would take the coach and he would ride along side on his hunter. She should have been grateful not to have to endure his company for the journey, as they'd never engaged in a conversation that hadn't ended in an argument, but part of her wished he'd traveled in the coach with her. He'd seemed so vulnerable the night before, so exposed when he talked about the girl he'd fallen for.

From the window, she watched him ride, proudly astride his horse against the backdrop of Sherwood Forest. To see him this morning, one would never have imagined him to be the same tortured man from the previous evening. He seemed so stoic, so confident, so noble, as he always did. She couldn't help but wonder about the identity of the girl who had captured his heart.

Did the girl have any inkling that he cared for her? Any idea at all? How sad to never know.

It was so odd thinking of the lieutenant as vulnerable in any way. For as long as she'd known him, he'd always seemed so strong, so austere. Of course, when she'd first met him her heart had fluttered. He was ruggedly handsome with green eyes that almost seemed to stare right into her soul. However, he'd hated her on sight, which had dulled his good looks considerably as far as she was concerned. But now all alone in the coach, Phoebe was afforded the opportunity to let her eyes linger on her one-time foe, and she was struck once again by how well he filled out his regimentals and how truly handsome he was. Any girl would be lucky to have his heart. He was honest, though often brutally so. He possessed a quick wit. He was honorable. He was everything Russell was not. Well, Russell *was* quick witted, but other than that, Tristan Avery was the by far the better specimen.

Seeing him now, it was easy to remember how he'd first stilled her heart. Of course, that was before he'd threatened to horsewhip her. A large Palladian home grew larger and larger out the window. In no time, the Avery coach stopped on the circle drive.

Tristan Avery dismounted from his steed and opened the carriage door, offering Phoebe his hand. "Miss Greywood."

Phoebe alighted from the conveyance and smiled when he tucked her hand in the crook of his arm. "Thank you."

He said nothing, but nodded as he led her along the stone path to Leverton Park's grand entrance. The large mahogany door opened as they reached the final step and the lieutenant guided Phoebe over the threshold. Her step hadn't faltered even once.

A pretty blonde stood in the foyer, her hands clasped before her, a radiant smile gracing her lips. "Tristan!" she gushed. "You've brought Miss Greywood, I presume."

The lieutenant inclined his head. "Amelia, this is Miss Phoebe Greywood. Miss Greywood, may I present Mrs. Amelia Moore."

Mrs. Moore's smile only widened as she stepped forward and linked her arm with Phoebe's. "I've heard so much about you." Her slight Welsh accent had a musical, lilting quality to it, making her seem kind and light-hearted at once.

Phoebe glanced up at the lieutenant who relinquished his hold on her. "I'm sure I'm much nicer than whatever he said."

Mrs. Moore laughed. "You are exactly as Cousin Cordie described." She tugged Phoebe further down the corridor. "Come this way and we'll acquaint ourselves."

"Speaking of Cordie," Lieutenant Avery began from behind them. "Where might I find my sister today?"

Mrs. Moore stopped in her tracks and frowned at the officer. "I'm afraid she's still abed, Tristan."

"Still not feeling well?"

"You should probably see her for yourself." She gestured to a footman a few feet away. "Murphy will take you to her room, if you'd like." Then she tilted her head toward Phoebe and said, "Let's go out to the lawn. The men are participating in a few games out of doors."

Phoebe glanced back at Lieutenant Avery one last

time before allowing Mrs. Moore to lead her down the corridor and around a corner.

"Cordie's not feeling well?" she asked after a moment.

Mrs. Moore tipped her head closer to Phoebe and whispered conspiratorially, "She's fairly certain she's increasing, but Clayworth is being overprotective, as usual."

Increasing? Again? Heavens, at this rate the Clayworths would have an entire brood before Phoebe found the right man, set her cap for him, was able to marry and start a family of her own. "He does tend to hover," she muttered instead of revealing her inner turmoil.

"We'll visit her later, once Tristan leaves her to join the others."

They entered a drawing room and the large ceiling to floor doors opened out onto the back lawn. A dozen or so men in regimentals littered the lawn and a few women and children were mingled together in small groups.

A few years ago, seeing a man in uniform like this would have sent Phoebe's heart all a flutter. But after Russell Avery, she figured it might be in her best interest to stay away from military men all together.

"I'm so glad you're here," Mrs. Moore said, her tone hushed as they stepped outside. "All of these women followed the drum and know each other rather well. I'm afraid I have nothing in common with any of them and I feel a bit like an outsider."

So did Phoebe, but mostly because she would never be one of them, even though she was the only one who knew that. "Then we shall have to band together," Phoebe promised.

"I knew I would like you. Cordie said we'd get along famously."

"She has never been wrong that I'm aware of, Mrs. Moore."

The blonde flashed a winning smile at Phoebe. "If we're to be the best of friends, you must call me Amelia."

"And you must call me Phoebe."

⁂

"How is life at Leverton Park, Murphy?" Tristan asked as the Irish infantryman turned footman led him up toward the family wing.

"A bit mad this week, Lieutenant, but otherwise, it's better than I'd hoped for."

Which Tristan was relieved to hear. Philip was to be commended for giving positions to out-of-work soldiers. A lot of noblemen could learn from his example. "Wonderful. I'm glad you've settled in well."

"And I'm grateful ta ye, sir, for findin' O'Leary an' me back in London."

"As am I." And equally grateful Murphy and O'Leary had volunteered to keep Philip safe when his life had been in danger.

After a few turns, the footman stopped in front of a chamber door and gestured to it. "Lady Clayworth's chamber."

"Thank you," Tristan said. When Murphy started back the way they'd come, Tristan rapped his knuckles against the door. "Cordie, are you awake?"

The door opened a half second later and Tristan was

surprised to find his brother-in-law looking so forlorn, his hair sticking up in all directions as though he had raked his hand through it a million times. Certainly, Cordie wasn't ill enough to warrant such panic. "What's the matter with her, Clayworth?"

"Nothing," Cordie grumbled from the four-poster in the middle of the room. "Brendan is being overly cautious."

Which hadn't ever been Tristan's opinion of the man, unless there was good reason. He stepped over the threshold, turning his full attention on his sister. "Has a doctor been called?"

Cordie heaved a sigh and pushed up on her arms to sit up against the headboard. "I'm simply not the best expectant lady, Tris. One would think my husband would remember that from the last time."

"The last time is a little foggy," Clayworth grumbled. "But I do recall Doctor Watts wanting you to stay in bed the last time."

Expectant? Tristan couldn't help grinning. He clapped his brother-in-law on the back. "Again? You don't waste any time, do you?"

"Tris," his sister complained. "Talk some sense into him, will you? I am perfectly capable of walking around Leverton Park and socializing with the other guests. Poor Amelia has never entertained like this before, you know, and—"

"When a doctor tells me you can get out of bed, I'll listen," Clayworth interrupted. "You've been green for two days and have barely kept any nourishment down. If I'd had any idea of your condition we'd have never come in the first place."

Cordie narrowed her eyes on the earl. "I love you with every breath I take, Brendan, but you are driving me mad."

Clayworth looked from his wife to Tristan. "Do you see how she is?"

"Don't know why you're surprised." Tristan laughed. "You knew she was stubborn and headstrong when you eloped with her." Then he crossed the room and sat on the edge of Cordie's bed. "How are you feeling, Cor?"

She winced a bit. "A little queasy to be honest."

Clayworth was right. She did have a greenish tint to her skin. "Then you probably should stay abed, don't you think?"

"I knew you'd take his side."

Tristan shook his head, grinning at his sister. "I'm on your side, like always." He squeezed her hand. "And I know you hate being cooped up, but if you're feeling queasy, you should wait until you're feeling better."

Her bottom lip thrust outward like it had when she was a little girl and hoped to persuade their father into something. It would serve her right to end up with a daughter just like her…

But then that thought struck pain in Tristan's heart. He wouldn't be around to see his new niece or nephew, would he? He'd missed so much while he was away and after he left to join the 16th, he'd miss everything else. Every birth, every holiday, every… wedding.

"Now *you* look green." Cordie leaned forward. "What's wrong, Tris?"

He couldn't tell her. She'd rant and rave and in her condition, that was hardly the best thing for anyone. So

Tristan shook his head instead. "Just worried about you."

Cordie blew the stray hair from her eyes in frustration. "Between you and Brendan…"

"Oh, yes." Tristan grinned as he tweaked her nose. "We're the evil villains, I know. We want you healthy and happy and—"

"I'd be happy if I could sit with Amelia and—" she sat taller "—Did Phoebe come today?"

"I brought her like you requested."

His sister's green eyes twinkled with joy. "You are my favorite brother, you know."

Clayworth clapped a hand to Tristan's back. "You've gone from evil villain to favorite brother in the matter of seconds."

"He's always been my favorite brother," Cordie protested. Then she batted her lashes at her husband. "Brendan, couldn't I at least go down to one of the parlors? I haven't seen Phoebe all summer and—"

"As though you'd let me have any peace if I said otherwise." Clayworth snorted. "I'll ring for your maid and then you can go down to one of the parlors if you promise to sit in one place."

"I solemnly swear." Cordie beamed, her smile lighting the room.

Fourteen

TRISTAN walked out onto Leverton's back lawn and immediately his eyes found Phoebe. Her head was tipped towards Amelia Moore's and the two of them giggled as though they'd been friends all their life and not just the half an hour of their acquaintance. She could brighten any gathering, just her presence.

"Ah," Philip said, limping toward Tristan with his cane. "I heard you were here."

Tristan pulled his eyes from Phoebe to Philip and smiled at his friend. "My sister is begging for Amelia's and Phoebe's company in your blue parlor. Clayworth says she can entertain them there if she'll sit still."

Philip's brow rose in amusement. "And she agreed to that?"

"Well, it was that or remain in her bed all day."

Philip nodded. "I can see why she took that deal then." His attention turned back to the crowd assembled on his lawn. "Did Russ come with you?"

Tristan snorted. "No. He tasked me with seeing to Miss Greywood today while he engages in his own entertainments."

Philip tilted his head toward Tristan. "Blackmailing you with something?"

"He's treated her so shabbily, I didn't put up much of a fight." His eyes once again sought out Phoebe. The sun made her hair shimmer with red and gold, and the breeze slightly lifted her tendrils from her face. What he wouldn't do to run his hands through her silken tresses.

"You always were the noblest of the Averys."

Hardly that. Tristan shrugged. "I don't have a lot of competition for that title, do I?" After all, Russell was a scoundrel of the first order and Greg had hardly been honorable throughout most of his life.

"You're one of the most noble men I know," Philip protested.

But a noble man wouldn't lust after his brother's fiancé. A noble man wouldn't have fallen in love with his brother's fiancé. Tristan was far from noble. "I'm sure I'm rotten to my Avery core just like my brothers." Then before his friend could ask him to explain that comment, Tristan said, "Excuse me, will you?" and crossed the lawn to where Phoebe and Amelia were still conversing.

Upon his approach, Phoebe looked up. Her blue eyes met his gaze, making his breath catch in his throat. She seemed to catch hers at the same time, and for the briefest of moments, Tristan wondered if it was possible that she could ever feel for him the way he did for her.

"Lieutenant." Phoebe smiled, which was rarely the case when she looked at him, and he felt it all the way to his soul.

"Miss Greywood, Mrs. Moore." He nodded his head in greeting. "My sister is begging for your company in the blue parlor."

"Oh!" Phoebe's face brightened even more. "Thank you."

Amelia linked her arm through Phoebe's and grinned at Tristan. "I'm certain you found her well."

"Well enough."

"Meaning Clayworth was vexing her?"

Tristan shook his head. "I dare say, Amelia, you will find Philip even more vexing when you are in a similar state."

A slight blush stained the blonde's cheeks. "Well, I hope so." Then she tugged Phoebe back toward the manor house, the two of them giggling like the silliest of schoolgirls.

He watched them leave a tried to swallow past the lump in his throat. Someday Philip would be the proudest father, doting on Amelia and their little ones. But Phoebe wouldn't be as fortunate with Russell. She deserved much better treatment than she'd receive, and the truth of that made rage boil in Tristan's veins once more.

From his position on the lawn, Philip caught Tristan's gaze, and the stoic major gestured for Tristan to join him. Though that was the last thing Tristan wanted to do, his feet seemed to have a mind of their own, and within a few moments, he was at his old friend's side.

"Why don't we head for my study?" Philip asked.

Tristan shook his head. "And suffer Amelia's annoyance again?"

"She'll be occupied with Cordie and Miss Greywood." He glanced back out at the lawn. "Besides everyone seems to be having a wonderful time. There's no need for us to stand guard. And I've got a very nice whisky Clayworth brought."

Whisky so early in the day? Philip clearly had something he wanted to say. So, Tristan agreed with a nod. "Why didn't you say so? After you, my old friend."

They entered the house and walked down the corridor, passing the blue parlor in the process. Phoebe's giggle reached Tristan's ears and he couldn't help but glance inside to steal one last look at her before he was sequestered in Philip's study.

His friend grunted, distracting Tristan from his intent and refocusing him on the path to the study. Once they'd arrived, Philip softly shut the door behind them and limped toward the sidebar against the far wall. He rested his cane against the edge and said, "A regular or a double?"

Tristan crossed the floor and leaned against the wall. "Depends on how long we'll be in here, I suppose."

"Double it is," Philip muttered, slightly swirling the contents of a crystal decanter as he picked it up. He splashed a healthy amount into a tumbler for Tristan and then poured one for himself that was equally full.

"What's on your mind?" Tristan asked as he retrieved his glass and started for one of the overstuffed chairs in front of Philip's desk.

"I could ask you the same question," his friend said, slowly making his way to his own chair. "Anything you want to tell me? Anything you want to get off your chest?"

Philip already knew about Canada. There was nothing left to tell. "No." He frowned at the major. "You know all my secrets."

"Do I?" Philip swallowed a bit of his whisky. Then he leaned back in his chair. "What's the real reason you want to join the 16th?"

Tristan shrugged. "I told you. Discovered I prefer to live abroad."

"And the situation has nothing to do with Phoebe Greywood?"

"Phoebe Greywood?" Tristan couldn't meet his friend's eyes, so he stared at the whisky in his tumbler as though it held the answers to all the questions in the universe.

"I saw the look on your face out there. You're in love with her," Philip said, a bit of surprise lacing his voice.

Tristan's gaze shot to his friend, to find the stoic major's dark eyes focused on him. Damn it all to hell. If Philip had figured him out so easily, the truth of the situation must be etched across Tristan's face. If he'd thought it would do him any good, he'd deny his friend's accusation; but Philip would clearly see right through him. "That obvious, is it?"

"And all this time I've been under the impression you couldn't abide the chit." Philip rubbed his brow as though he was suddenly plagued with a headache. "Does Russ know?"

At that, Tristan couldn't help but snort. Philip might have sorted Tristan out, but Russell was so singularly focused on his own divertissements, Tristan could have taken to the stage and professed his love for his brother's betrothed in rhyming measure and verse and Russell wouldn't be any the wiser. "Does he pay any notice to anyone other than himself?"

"That's not entirely fair," Philip replied.

No, it wasn't. But Damn Philip for saying as much. For most of his life, Russell hadn't just been Tristan's brother, he'd also been his best friend. Tristan lifted his glass to his lips and took a healthy swallow.

"What are you going to do?" Philip placed his drink on the desk before him.

A mirthless laugh escaped Tristan. "I can't stay here, can I? I can't bear witness to this union on a daily basis. Russ doesn't love her and she deserves better."

"Meaning you."

"Hardly." Tristan snorted again. "I certainly wouldn't bring luster to her name."

"And how does she feel about the situation?"

Tristan gaped at his friend as though he'd sprouted a second nose. "How the devil should I know that?"

"So, you haven't talked to her about this, then?"

Not in any real way. He certainly hadn't confessed that the girl he'd fallen for was *her*. Tristan shook his head. "What am I to say, Moore? She's to be my bloody sister. My *sister* for God's sake. Should I tap on her door and say, 'I know you're betrothed to my brother, but why don't we run away together instead? How do you feel about Canada?' Because we certainly couldn't stay here. She'd be ruined, ostracized. Can you imagine?"

"No." Philip shook his head. "No, I cannot. You need to find a way to put her out of your mind, Tris."

Out of his mind or out of his heart? "Don't you think I've tried? She's… she's ever present in my thoughts, like an infernal tune I can't escape."

Philip's brows rose in what looked like surprise. "I'd stay away from odes, were I you."

Odes were the least of his troubles. "I suppose if I thought Russ loved her, it would be different. I... it *would* be different," Tristan insisted. "But he doesn't care anything for her, as you well know. He's so busy skirt chasing, he hasn't given her a second thought since we returned home." Tristan raked a hand through his hair. "Well, until now that she's under our bloody roof. You should see her, seeking his attention, his damned affection, but he could care less."

Philip's frown deepened. "He jumped into this betrothal rather hastily. Perhaps he's regretting his impulsivity."

It didn't matter if he was. Russell couldn't cry off, and she didn't seem likely to. Not the way she batted her eyes in Russ' direction whenever he was near. "I can't sit back and watch it, Philip. I just can't."

"So you'll run off to Canada, then? Leave your family and friends and your life behind?"

He didn't care a thing about Canada. Not really. "Have you a better suggestion?"

Philip rose from his spot, leaning heavily on his cane. "I do know a thing or two about losing the woman you love, you know." Then he rested his hip on the edge of his desk, looking down on Tristan as their instructors did at Harrow all those years ago.

"Olivia didn't marry your brother." It was hardly the same thing at all.

"No, I haven't a brother."

"And if she had married *Russ*?"

"She has better taste than that."

Despite himself, Tristan grinned. "I know you were devastated by her loss, Philip; but now you have Amelia and…"

"And that's how I know you'll find the right girl for you, Tris. Like I did."

Tristan shook his head.

"I know you think such a thing is impossible. I did too, you might remember. But then Amelia…"

"Thawed your frozen heart. I know. But it's not the same thing, my friend."

Philip frowned once more. "Because Russell will always be your brother."

"And because I will always love her. I don't seem to have a choice in the matter." Tristan downed the rest of his whisky in one gulp. "Sometimes," he began, his eyes stinging just a bit, "I think it would have been easier if I'd never returned from the battlefields."

A hardened look settled on his friend's face. "Many good men didn't, Tris. And I wouldn't trade you for any one of them. Don't wish yourself away so cavalierly."

It was an awful thing to say to Philip, considering the man barely returned from Belgium with his life. Tristan forced a smile to his face. "Sorry to be so maudlin."

"I'm sure I've been so myself more than once over the last few years."

Fifteen

"I AM so happy for you," Phoebe gushed, embracing Cordie tightly. It truly was so wonderful to see her friend again. Hearing happy news only made their reunion better.

Her friend hugged her back and then said, "Sit, sit! I haven't heard from you in forever, Phoebe Greywood."

No, she hadn't. "I am sorry." But Phoebe hadn't known what to pen in a letter to her friend about her predicament. No matter how wonderful their friendship was, Cordie was and always would be Russell's sister. So it had been easier not to say anything at all. She settled in beside Cordie on the settee as Amelia Moore took a spot in a chintz chair across from them.

"You should be." Cordie frowned. "How can I help you, if you won't tell me what is happening with you?"

"Help me?" Phoebe shook her head. "You orchestrated this whole thing, didn't you? Major Moore's house party? My family's invitation to Rufford

Hall?"

Unrepentantly, Cordie shrugged. "Of course. Should I have waited for Russell to do something instead? I'd be waiting a very long time to see you, if that was the case, and since you weren't writing me, you left me very little choice."

"I do adore Captain Avery," Amelia put in softly. "I might never have met my Philip if not for him. I owe him a debt that can never be repaid, but Cordie says he hasn't been the best fiancé to you, which I understand better than most. We only want to help."

"And now that Brendan is insisting we return to Bayhurst Court this week due to my condition, I won't be around much longer to help," Cordie complained.

What had Amelia Moore said? Russell hadn't been the best fiancé? That was an understatement of monumental proportions. The major's wife must be quite close for Cordie to divulge such information, but as she already seemed to know—and it also seemed that the two had concocted this entire event together—there was no point in lying about it. Phoebe heaved a sigh. "After much thought and consideration, I don't believe we'll suit. I'm going to cry off."

Cordie gasped, and her hand flew to her mouth. "Phoebe! It can't be as bad as all that."

Phoebe narrowed her eyes on the meddling countess. "Don't tell me you haven't heard the same stories about him that I have—"

"I don't believe every rumor that—"

"If even half of them are true, if even a *fourth* of them are true, Cordie, I couldn't go through with this marriage."

Cordie grasped Phoebe's hand and squeezed, her expression so very pained. "Phoeb, you know as well as I that stories have a way of being stretched to sound more… fantastical."

"I know you wanted us to be sisters, Cordie." Phoebe frowned at her friend. "I wanted that too. But if you were me, you wouldn't want this life."

"No, I wouldn't." Cordie's grasp tightened on Phoebe's hand. "If I were you, I would have done something foolish like set my cap for the wrong fellow and then elope with the right one."

Phoebe couldn't help but laugh. "That's exactly what you *did* do."

Her friend finally smiled. "Well, it turned out for the best, didn't it?"

It had turned out perfectly. Cordie had ended up with a wonderful man who loved her immensely. She was able to escape out from the clutches of her evil mother. And for all intents and purposes, she was living happily ever after, even if her doting husband did dote too much on occasion. "And I'm so happy it did."

"You haven't told Russ yet, have you?"

Phoebe shook her head. "But I won't change my mind, if that's what you're hoping."

"No." Cordie heaved a sigh. "I don't expect you will. Are you waiting until the end of your stay at Rufford Hall?"

"That seems to make the most sense. I'd rather not set the place on its ear in the meantime."

"My mother will have an apoplexy, I'm sure. Russ is her favorite. You're wise to wait until the last moment."

Lady Avery. Just the mention of the woman made

Phoebe's stomach twist in a knot. "I have been trying my best to keep my distance from her."

The expression in Cordie's eyes was at once haunted, as though remembering less happy times in her life. "I'm certain you have nothing to fear from her other than aching ears once she starts her wailing."

Phoebe didn't imagine Lady Avery would try to harm her as she'd done Cordie. For one thing, Papa would never stand for it, and Phoebe would never keep such a thing a secret as Cordie had done. Still, perhaps she should spend as much time as possible with Papa or Matthew in the upcoming days just to be safe. "I'd rather focus on something else. Have you started thinking of names?"

"Names?" Cordie laughed. "We have not thought that far ahead yet."

"Oh, Cordie," Amelia began. "Philip wanted me to ask, have you heard anything about Miss Kelly?"

A frown marred the countess' face. "I sent her a letter with funds, asking her to come stay with me, but I haven't heard a word from her. Brendan even sent a man to Dublin to see if he could find the girl."

"Who is Miss Kelly?" Phoebe asked.

"The sister to one of the fellows Tristan hired to keep watch over Philip and Amelia last summer. Her brother was killed in the process and I promised to see to the girl, but I haven't had any luck."

"That's awful." Phoebe touched a hand to her heart.

"I'm not giving up," Cordie declared. "She has to be somewhere and wherever that is, I'll find her."

And Phoebe had no doubt she would be successful. Cordie always accomplished anything she set her mind to.

"But for now, let's talk of something happier, shall we?"

"Like little bundles of joy?" Phoebe suggested.

"Oh! I think we should celebrate!" Amelia said, rising from her spot and clapping her hands together. "What shall we have?"

"Nothing for me." Cordie groaned. "The idea of anything but a bit of bread makes me queasy, but the two of you are welcome to celebrate my good news any way you'd like."

"We'll get you some bread and maybe a spot of tea?" Amelia suggested.

"Such a celebration," Cordie muttered which made Phoebe giggle.

Amelia started toward the bellpull. "It's better than not celebrating at all." Then she smiled at Phoebe. "What would you like to drink? Madeira? Or Brandy?"

Phoebe shrugged. "I've never had brandy."

"Then we must rectify that this instant." After Amelia tugged on the bellpull, she poured what must be brandy into a pair of glasses. Then she crossed the floor and handed one of them to Phoebe. "You'll love it."

Phoebe looked down at the dark amber drink and wrinkled her nose. She never imbibed in spirits except for an occasional glass of wine with dinner.

"Do drink it," Cordie complained. "The smell is getting to me."

Phoebe lifted the glass to her lips and downed it one gulp. It tasted sweet and heavy, warming her mouth, throat and even her belly. She coughed.

"I didn't mean to guzzle it." Cordie smothered a

laugh.

"You said the smell—" Phoebe coughed again "—was getting to you."

"And you are the dearest friend to down it all at once." Cordie lost her apparent battle with holding in her laughter.

Phoebe scowled at her friend. "I'm glad you find me so amusing." Heavens her mouth was even warmer than it had been a few moments ago. "That stuff is horrid."

"You're supposed to drink it slowly," Amelia said, swirling her brandy around in her glass. "Let it breathe a bit."

A silver haired butler cleared his throat from the doorway. "You rang, madam?"

Amelia dropped back into her seat and smiled at the old man. "Yes, Wilson. We'd like some tea and biscuits, please. And some bread for Lady Clayworth too."

The butler nodded, then disappeared back into the corridor.

Amelia turned her attention back to Phoebe. "Pour yourself another. We haven't toasted Cordie yet."

The last thing Phoebe wanted was more brandy, but she pushed to her feet anyway. As she made her way to the sideboard, warmth began to spread across her limbs, which was an interesting sensation and not all together unpleasant. She poured herself a bit more of the drink, not quite as full as Amelia had poured the first glass, then she made her way back to the settee.

Amelia lifted her glass and said, "To the newest Reese addition, boy or girl. You will have the best parents in the world."

"Aww." Cordie blushed a bit.

Phoebe lifted her glass. "And to Cordelia Clayworth. Though you won't be my sister, you'll always be my dearest friend."

Cordie slid across the settee and wrapped her arms around Phoebe in a hug. "I love you." Then she pulled back and winced. "Forget what I said before about going slow. Drink the rest of that, the smell is turning my stomach."

Phoebe raised her brow in annoyance. She'd just been laughed at for that very thing. Still she lifted the brandy to her lips and drank again, though this time it went down much smoother and she decided she quite liked the warmth that came with the drink. It made her feel tingly and happy. Another drink, if she wasn't so close to Cordie and her delicate nose, might just be in order.

Sixteen

PEALS of laughter spilled into the main corridor, and the sound only grew louder the longer Tristan and Philip stood at the end.

Tristan turned his head toward his friend. "What the devil are they doing in there?"

Philip chuckled. "I'd wager they're having a wonderful time."

That was an understatement. "Well, I hate to break it up, but I have to get her home." He strode toward the blue parlor and stepped over the threshold. Phoebe, Amelia and Cordie were all laughing so hard and holding their sides, they didn't even notice him enter the room.

Tristan shook his head and couldn't keep from smiling. Such an abundance of levity was, apparently, contagious. "What is so amusing?" he asked.

At once a collective gasp echoed throughout the

room, and a startled Amelia slid from her chair onto the floor. All three ladies erupted in laughter once more at the same time Philip limped into the parlor as well.

"Good God," Tristan muttered, not that anyone other than Philip heard him as the ladies' giggles completely drowned him out.

"Oh, Philip!" Amelia pushed back up into her chair, or attempted to anyway, and then slid back to the ground.

"Amelia!" Philip sucked in a breath when his wife tumbled back to the floor.

Tristan crossed the room in three strides and offered his hand to Amelia Moore. "Do let me help you."

She grinned up at him, her blue eyes shiny like glass. "Th-thank you, Tristan," she slurred as he pulled her back to her feet. She wasn't steady, however, and she smelled like she'd bathed in brandy. What in the world were they doing in here all afternoon?

Tristan frowned as he guided Amelia back to the chintz chair she had been sitting in until his arrival. "Don't move," he warned as Philip made his way toward his wife's seat. Then Tristan turned his glare to the settee where Phoebe and Cordie continued to giggle like schoolgirls. "Are you *all* deep in your cups?" he demanded.

"Not me." Cordie shook her head. "I'm sober as vicar."

Tristan knew a number of vicars who imbibed on a regular basis. "That means very little."

Cordie rolled her eyes heavenward. "We are celebrating my good news, Tris. There's no reason to look like a storm cloud."

At least she sounded sober.

Phoebe snorted. "He always—" she over enunciated each syllable and her blue eyes widened as though that would help her sober up "—looks like a storm cloud."

"Good God," Tristan groaned louder than he had before. It was past time for them to have started back for Rufford Hall, and he couldn't take her home like *this*. "Her father is going to kill me."

Cordie shook her head. "Since he hasn't killed Russell yet, I'm sure you're safe."

What was that supposed to mean? Tristan frowned. "I'm already supposed to have her in the carriage headed for home."

"I don't want to go," Phoebe declared. "I'll just stay here."

Tristan scoffed. "There's no room at the inn." He was, after all, well aware of that fact.

"I beg your pardon?" Phoebe blinked her azure eyes at him.

"Come on," he grumbled, stepping toward the settee and thrusting his hand in Phoebe's direction.

A giggle escaped her. "I don't think I can walk, Lieutenant." A giggle escaped her, which set off the other two ladies as well. "I'll just stay here in *this* parlor for the next fortnight."

"That's not an option." Tristan bent down and scooped her up in his arms, eliciting a gasp from the lady in the process. Holding her against his chest wasn't the wisest course of action as desire raced to his nether regions. God help him if anyone else in the parlor noticed.

Phoebe's eyes locked with his and her mouth fell

open. "I can walk. Put me down."

Tristan scoffed. "If Amelia can't even sit, I don't think there's any hope for *you* walking. Now put your arms around my neck."

She did as he asked, her delicate arms wrapping around him. If it wasn't for the scowl she cast him, Tristan would have enjoyed the experience much more.

He strode toward the corridor, nodding once in Philip's direction. "See you soon." Then he carried Phoebe down the hallway and out the front doors into the waning afternoon light.

The Avery coach awaited them and Tristan called to the driver, "Get the door and leave my horse. I'll have to come back for it tomorrow."

The coachman hastened from his box, opening the carriage door so quickly Tristan didn't have to slow his pace. He dropped onto a bench, never losing his hold on Phoebe.

Her arms slid from around his neck. "You can put me down, Lieutenant."

He could, but when would he ever get the chance to hold her like this again? He did have many cold nights in Canada ahead of him, after all. "And watch you fall to the floor like Amelia?" He shook his head. "You are foxed." Tristan adjusted the bundle in his arms.

"And *you* are mean," she replied as her eyes drifted shut and her head fell against his shoulder. "Sobriety will return to *me* in the morning."

Mean? She thought he was mean? No matter that she was his brother's intended or that it might be better if she did think he was mean to keep some distance between them, Tristan hated to think that she thought so lowly of him. "You're the only one who thinks I'm mean," he said, trying to keep a jovial tone to his voice.

She scoffed. "You threatened to horsewhip me." Her adorable bottom lip jutted out in a pout. What Tristan wouldn't do taste that lip, just once. "That wasn't very nice."

Dear God, that was two years ago. Wasn't there some statute of limitations on his *crime*? At the time he'd have said anything to have Cordie returned safely home. "You *had* helped a scoundrel abscond with my sister," he reminded her.

Phoebe opened her pretty eyes, which were rounded more than normal in her inebriated state. Goddamn it, she was the most beautiful sight he'd ever seen. Damn Russell to hell for capturing Phoebe Greywood before Tristan realized he loved her, before Tristan realized his heart beat a little faster whenever she was near.

"I did," she agreed softly, breaking him from his inner cursing of his brother's name. "And I would do it again too, Lieutenant."

Tristan frowned at the pretty bundle in his arms as the coach lurched forward. "I'm not sure Clayworth would appreciate your interference, Miss Greywood. You might want to reconsider."

She rolled her eyes, which must have been a chore considering her drunkenness. "She doesn't need to escape Lord Clayworth. I always told her he was a better match, anyway. But she didn't listen to me. Not that it mattered. She's my friend and I would have helped her in any way possible."

Escape? That made no sense at all. Gibberish, Tristan supposed, was what one got when one tried to converse with a lady deep in her cups. But it was so rare that he got to converse with Phoebe Greywood, he couldn't quite keep himself from wanting to talk about anything, about everything, as long as she looked at him with those pretty azure eyes.

"You make it sound as though she was in trapped some tower, guarded by a dragon." He quirked her with, what he'd been told on more than one occasion was, his most charming smile.

She sat forward in his arms, her face a hairsbreadth away from his. Her brandy scented breath blew across his lips. "It was worse than that," she whispered as though she feared someone would overhear her.

"Worse than being trapped in a tower guarded by a dragon?" Who knew Miss Greywood was so disposed to the theatrical?

"I don't know how you can stand to be in the same room with that woman."

With Cordie? Tristan shook his head, trying to make sense of Miss Greywood's words. "I'm related to her, but she's your friend," he reminded her good-naturedly.

Horror flashed across her face. "Friend?" her voice raised an octave. "I can't even look at her or shivers race down my spine like a ghost touched me."

Definitely a flair for the dramatic. "I know you don't mean that." Miss Greywood should keep her distance from brandy in the future. And the stage. Of course with her balance she'd probably fall into the pit.

But she nodded her head most insistently. "I most certainly do. Marrying into your family has given me nightmares on more than one occasion, but I didn't think Russell would let her hurt me. Do you?"

"Why should Cordie ever want to hurt you? You're one of her dearest friends. But I think she would be hurt if she ever heard you say such things about her."

A frown marred Miss Greywood's startled face. "Cordie?"

"Isn't that who we've been talking about?"

"Were we?" She blinked her blue eyes innocently, her lashes brushing against her cheeks. "I don't think I was." Confusion settled on her face as though her brandy soaked mind was trying to make sense of their conversation.

"Whom were you speaking about then?" Tristan asked.

Miss Greywood leaned forward, so close he thought she might kiss him, but she grazed his cheek with hers as she whispered in his ear. "Lady Avery."

Mother? Tristan held in a snort. His mother wasn't the warmest woman, but she wasn't a dragon either, not even the sort one often found in society. She was more of a sycophant to societal dragons, honestly. "Mother can be difficult to reason with, but—"

Her lips touched his ear and desire shot straight to Tristan's loins. He couldn't even breathe and his arms tightened around her.

"She's awful," Miss Greywood insisted. "Please don't tell her I got foxed."

Tristan hadn't planned on telling anyone, his mother included. But he couldn't understand why Miss Greywood seemed so terrified of his mother. "Has she done something to you?"

Miss Greywood shook her head and then frowned as though she wished she hadn't moved so rapidly.

Clearly, his mother had done something to frighten the girl. "Miss Greywood, you must tell me what she's done."

The color drained from Miss Greywood's face. "I swore I would never tell a soul."

That was on the outside of enough. If his mother had done something so egregious that Phoebe Greywood was terrified of her, someone ought to know what that thing was. "I insist you tell me, Miss Greywood. So I can prevent her from ever doing whatever it is again."

But she shook her head again. "I don't think Lord Clayworth would let her hurt Cordie again." Then her eyes widened and she covered her mouth with her hand as though she shouldn't have said those words aloud.

"Hurt Cordie?" he whispered in return.

"You think Russell would protect me from her, don't you?"

Russell. Just his brother's name was like a dagger to Tristan's heart. "If he won't, I will," he vowed, though he had no idea what she was talking about. Was it still the brandy?

"But you'll be in Canada," she said, her azure eyes boring into his, making Tristan's heart ache.

※

The look of torture on Lieutenant Avery's face squeezed Phoebe's heart, reminding her of their late-night conversation in the library. "I am sorry." She touched her fingers to his cheek.

He tilted his head into her hand, like a dog who wanted to be stroked. Phoebe couldn't help but comply, brushing her fingers across his cheek, exploring his strong jaw, touching his bottom lip.

Tristan's green eyes widened in surprise, then they closed when he captured her hand and kissed her palm.

Something, Phoebe wasn't certain what, filled her with more warmth than the brandy had done. A soft moan escaped her and the lieutenant's eyes opened, spearing her with his tortured look once more.

"What are you doing, Phoebe?" he whispered.

"I'm not sure," she replied. And she wasn't. It was difficult to put more than two thoughts together at the moment. The world, the carriage, Tristan, all seemed to blend together, lulling her like she'd never been, but she didn't want it to end and she wanted to be all warm and tingly. So she pressed against him, slid her hands to his neck, and pressed her lips to his.

The warmth she craved washed over her and she sighed happily, her eyes fluttering closed. Tristan's arm tightened around her, and he kissed her back. He sucked at her bottom lip and groaned as thought it had been ripped from him. Phoebe felt the sound as though it was inside her, echoing in her heart and in her core.

His tongue slid inside her mouth and the warmth inside Phoebe turned to heat. She touched her tongue to his and reveled when he groaned again, more urgently this time. Her fingers toyed with the hair at the nape of his neck, and his fingers possessively tightened their grip on her back.

"God, Phoebe," he whispered across her lips before delving back inside her mouth.

His kiss was like heaven, like the balm for everything that had caused her pain. It was euphoric and heady and all consuming. Tears of joy threatened to spill down her cheeks.

"Tell me you're too foxed to remember this tomorrow," he said softly before trailing his lips from her mouth to her neck.

She'd never forget this, not if she lived to be a hundred, but she didn't want say anything that would make him stop. "I'm too foxed to remember this tomorrow," she lied.

"Good." His gravelly voice washed over her, making her whole body pulse with need. His hand moved from her back across her stomach and up toward her breasts. He captured one and squeezed, then kneaded her softly.

Her nipples peaked, straining against her chemise, and Phoebe thought she might die if he didn't touch her there. She peppered his temple and brow with urgent kisses, pressing herself closer and closer to him. And then one of his fingers dipped beneath her décolletage, brushing against one of her nipples. Phoebe sucked in her breath.

He caressed her, toyed with her, lightly pinched her and she was certain she'd unravel right there in his arms. "Oh, Tristan," she breathed.

"I love you," he whispered. "I've always loved you." Then his mouth sought hers once more.

She kissed him in return and clutched his jacket in her hands to steady herself as he plundered her mouth and invaded her senses and made her more carefree than she'd ever been.

Seventeen

TRISTAN paced the drawing room, his hands clutched behind his back. He was the worst sort of cad. He'd taken advantage of her, of his goddamned brother's fiancée. He'd taken advantage of her and she'd been too foxed to know the difference. There was a special place in hell for him, he was sure.

"Phoebe's not feeling well?" Russell asked from the other side of the room, breaking Tristan from his self-berating, bringing his attention to the fact that the drawing room was filled with both his family and the Greywoods.

When had the others arrived?

Tristan forced a smile to his face. "She's resting." Sleeping off the effects of her over-imbibing and hopefully forgetting the entire carriage ride back to Rufford Hall. Dear God, he'd never forget that ride — the breathy way she said his name, the feel of her tongue toying with his, the way her breast filled his hand.

"Didn't you say Cordie wasn't feeling well the day before?" Greg asked from his spot against the doorjamb.

"Oh, I hope whatever it is isn't catching," Mrs. Greywood declared, her hand settling near her heart.

Tristan shook his head. "Phoebe couldn't catch what ails Cordie." Though that wasn't necessarily true, was it? Had the carriage ride been longer, he might have had her skirts lifted up around her waist, cad that he apparently was.

"What ails Cordie?" Russell asked, a frown marring his brow.

Tristan shrugged, hoping to shake all thoughts of Phoebe from his mind. "It's not so much what *ails* her, but it's not really my secret to tell."

"She's increasing again," his mother grumbled. "Isn't she?"

That was odd. Shouldn't their mother be glad to welcome another grandchild into the world? Phoebe's cryptic statements about his mother echoed in Tristan's mind. "How did you know?"

His mother didn't reply, just scowled a bit. No one else noticed, however, as a chorus of happy gasps resounded from everyone else.

"That is wonderful!" Greg said, stepping further into the drawing room. "We shall have to celebrate tonight."

Phoebe had celebrated enough for all of them, though Tristan resisted the urge to mention that.

"Agreed." Russell grinned. "Now she'll be too busy to try and manage me."

"And me," Greg added. "But I'm happy for her, just the same. She does love motherhood."

"Clayworth must be thrilled," Mr. Greywood chimed in.

"He's got his hands full trying to keep her abed," Tristan told them. "You know Cordie, always exuberant, always full of life."

"A handful. Too spirited," his mother grumbled. "He should take a firmer hand with her."

"I think he loves her just the way she is," Greg replied warningly, which was odd. Why should Greg have such a tone?

"Well," Russell began, starting toward the corridor, "since Phoebe isn't joining us, we should all head into dinner, shouldn't we?" Not a note of concern sounded in his voice about his ill fiancée. The unfeeling blackguard.

※

Phoebe still tingled all the way to her toes, and she knew without a doubt, it wasn't the brandy.

He loved her. He said he'd always loved her. She stared at the ceiling above her, not even able to blink. He loved *her*. She still couldn't believe it. Lieutenant Tristan Avery loved her and he kissed her like he meant it. His touch so strong yet tender was the most amazing thing she'd ever felt against her skin.

She'd always been convinced that he hated her. He'd always acted as though he hated her. But their late-night conversation in the library echoed once more in her brandy-soaked mind. Hadn't he said he'd fallen in love when he retuned from the continent? That didn't speak to *always*, did it? Of course not.

So had he fallen in love with someone else?

Perhaps she misheard him? Perhaps he misspoke? But if so, when? Last night? Or caught up in their passion that afternoon?

Last night he said the girl he loved belonged to another fellow, that she found Tristan reprehensible. That's why he was headed to Canada. He couldn't stop loving her no matter how he tried.

But what if he didn't mean *her*? What if he was truly in love with someone else and Phoebe had been a diversion? Her heart ached at the thought. Somehow that possibility had the potential to hurt her much more deeply than Russell's lack of affection had done.

But what if he *did* mean her? What if he left for Canada, never to see her again? And all because he thought she held him in contempt? All because of her soon-to-be ended betrothal to Captain Avery?

She sat bolt upright in bed, swamped in panic. She could never live with herself if he fled England because of her. She had to know the truth. She had to know for certain if he loved her or some other girl, and if the latter was true, she'd have to find a way to mend her heart that she hadn't realized until now beat for him.

Yet it was true.

Every barb he'd sent her direction, every one she'd cast in his, they'd all been laced with… something, hadn't they? Something she hadn't understood 'til now, something she hadn't known to give a name to. But it was true. There had always been a connection between them, a pull that neither of them of wanted to acknowledge.

She touched a hand to her lips that still remembered the pressure of his. How incredibly foolish she'd been not to see it earlier. If he felt the same, she couldn't let him flee to Canada. She just couldn't.

Dinner was in full swing, but she could sneak down to the library, couldn't she? That seemed to be where she usually bumped into him, his sanctuary from his family, it seemed.

Her mind made up, Phoebe tossed her legs over the side of the bed and pushed to her feet. The room spun a bit, but she regained her balance. She lifted the hem of her gown to keep from tripping and carefully padded toward the doorway. She stumbled forward anyway, and was glad Tristan hadn't been around to see it.

※

Lord Avery had a rather large assortment on mythology. Roman, Greek, Norse. Phoebe retrieved a leather volume from the shelf and then settled onto the settee, preparing to wait as long as it took for Tristan to arrive. And he would come, she knew it. She knew it as well as she knew she needed air to breathe.

Soon she was engrossed in the tome, flipping page after page, caught up in the middle of Psyche's tortured love story with Cupid. When someone cleared his throat from the threshold, Phoebe dropped the book in her haste to rise.

"Tristan…" She tried to cover up her disappointment at finding Russell there instead. "Oh, Captain Avery." She feigned a smile for his benefit.

The regal officer stepped further into the library, a look of chagrin on his face. "You were expecting my brother?"

"I…" Phoebe shook her head. "No, I…um…That is, usually when someone interrupts me in a library it's Lieutenant Avery," she lied.

Russell chuckled. "That is Tristan. He often has his

nose in one book or another." He crossed the floor in a few strides and offered her his hand. "I was worried about you when you didn't come down to dinner."

The liar. But the heat in Phoebe's conviction had dulled since her arrival at Rufford Hall. Russell wasn't the man for her. There was no reason to wish him ill over it, not when she should be counting her lucky stars that she discovered his duplicity before oaths were spoken. "I thought a book would help me fall asleep."

"Might you give me a few moments of your time before you run off to your chambers?"

"Of course," she muttered quietly.

He smiled, reminding her of the handsome captain she'd first fallen for. How silly she'd been, just like Psyche, letting a man's handsome looks distract her from what was truly important. "Let's sit, shall we?" He gestured to the settee behind her.

Phoebe took a spot on the settee and smiled when Captain Avery retrieved her book from the floor and handed it to her. "Thank you."

He nodded, then assumed the place beside her. "I do hope you'll forgive me for neglecting you this afternoon."

"I'm certain you had something of import that had your attention." The question was whether or not it was a blonde or brunette.

"Still—" he took her hand in his "—it was unforgivable. I'm afraid my brother has reprimanded me for my lack of attention."

Tristan? The idea pained her heart more than a bit. "I'm surprised Lieutenant Avery gave me any thought," she said, hoping her disappointment wasn't obvious.

At that Russell Avery laughed. "Tristan? He berated me all summer. No, Gregory lectured me at length today. He…uh….made it very clear what was expected of me and that I had been found lacking thus far." He grinned again. "I am glad to find you in here tonight, Phoebe. I know you wanted us to reacquaint ourselves after my return from Belgium. And you were right. Why don't we do so now?" He leaned toward her and pressed his lips to hers.

But it was wrong, *he* was wrong. She pushed against his chest at the same moment he wrapped his arms around her.

"Pardon me," came an all too familiar voice from the threshold.

Tristan.

Phoebe recoiled, pressing herself against the far corner of the settee, her eyes darting to the doorway only to find it empty. She turned her fury on her fiancé. "What *are* you doing?"

Russell's brow rose in surprise. "It's not as though you haven't kissed me before, Phoebe."

Yes, when she'd been foolish and thought herself in love with him, but now… And Tristan had seen that blasted kiss, she was sure of it. Phoebe shook her head. "I'm afraid the time to reacquaint ourselves has passed us, Captain." She stumbled to her feet, almost losing her balance.

"I beg your pardon?" He frowned.

But Phoebe didn't have time to deal with him. Not now, not with Tristan headed… somewhere, and she had to catch him. She darted toward the doorway.

Eighteen

TRISTAN shouldn't have stayed at Rufford Hall. As soon as he learned the Greywoods had been invited, he should have turned on his heel and started back for London. But he'd stayed. Some part of him needed to see Phoebe again no matter that it was the wrong thing to do. He certainly shouldn't have kissed her, and he certainly had no right to be angry at finding her in a passionate embrace with Russell. The two were betrothed, after all. She didn't belong to Tristan and she never would.

A knock sounded on his door and Tristan glared at it as though it was an approaching enemy line.

"Open the damn door!" Russell barked.

Tristan snorted. "It's not locked. Open it yourself."

A half-second later, the door banged open and his enraged brother entered the room, huffing like an angry bull. "Where is she?"

Had a chambermaid escaped his brother? Or had

Russell simply lost his mind? "Where is who?"

Russ' green eyes narrowed to little slits. "Don't play me for a fool. I know she ran after you. Where is she?"

Tristan gaped at his brother. "Russell, I have no idea what you're talking about."

"Phoebe," Russell ground through his teeth. "Is she hiding in your wardrobe? Under your bed? Where is she?"

"Phoebe?" Tristan echoed. "*Phoeb*e ran after me?" Had she really? His heart lifted a bit at the thought, though it had no right to. "The chit can barely walk and you actually saw her *run*?"

Russell stalked toward Tristan, his green eyes ablaze. "Sorry to have interrupted your little tête-à-tête with *my* fiancé, but what have you done with her?"

Tête-à-tête? *Now* Russell gave a damn about Phoebe? Why? Because he thought someone else was interested in her? Or because she was simply in residence? "Did you drink all the port in the cellar?"

"Are you denying that you set up a rendezvous with Phoebe this evening?"

"I am denying it." That was a question Tristan could answer honestly. "I did no such thing."

Russell glared at him, studying him as though assessing Tristan's truthfulness. "She was expecting *you* in the library," Russell accused. "And then when you showed up, she ran after you."

Had she really run after him? He'd left at such a pace, she'd have never caught him and she certainly didn't know which chamber belonged to him. "Perhaps she was just running from you," Tristan replied evenly.

His brother scoffed at the ridiculousness of that

statement. "And why would she do that?"

"Perhaps someone told her where you really spent your day while she was off visiting Amelia and our sister," he suggested.

"Oh, here we are once more. Saint Tristan." Russell's eyes blazed with fire. "You haven't been the same ever since we returned from Belgium."

Tristan agreed with the nod of his head. "But you're the same as you've always been, aren't you? I've just grown up is all."

"Gone soft is more like it." Russell shoved Tristan's chest. "How I conduct myself and with whom is none of your concern and certainly none of hers. If I find out you told her where I was—"

Tristan didn't even realize he'd balled up his fist until he'd crashed it into his brother's jaw. But as Russell fell backwards, he grabbed Tristan's jacket and they both fell to the floor in a heap. Russell managed to roll on top, and he smashed his fist into Tristan's eye.

Tristan roared, shoving his brother off him. Then he scrambled to his knees and got in two good shots to Russell's stomach.

His brother kicked, connecting with Tristan's chest. He fell backward against his wardrobe, which swayed to the side and then crashed onto the rug with a loud thud. But Tristan didn't pay it any attention. Russell was scrambling back to his feet, and Tristan grabbed his brother's jacket, pulling him back to the floor.

Just as he got off another punch to Russell's jaw…

"What in God's name is going on in here?" Greg demanded from the corridor. Then he crossed the threshold, glaring at his brothers.

Russell was the first to find his feet and he dusted his hands on his trousers, though his enraged eyes never left Tristan. "Nothing that concerns you, Greg."

Tristan pushed back to his feet, his breaths coming out in ragged pants. "Just a disagreement."

"Just a disagreement?" Greg echoed incredulously. "Do you have any idea of the racket you've made? How am I to explain that to the Greywoods?"

"You're the one worried about propriety," Russell growled. "So tell them whatever you damn well want."

A muscle twitched near Greg's eye. "I don't know what's going on with the two of you, but it ends now."

Tristan shook his head. "No need for threats, Greg. I'm leaving for London in the morning."

"London?" Russell growled.

"London," Tristan echoed. "And then I'm joining the 16th in Canada. So you can manage your own life and your farce of a betrothal anyway you see fit from here on out." Because God knew Tristan couldn't stay around any longer to watch the disaster that was Russell and Phoebe for one moment longer. His heart couldn't take it.

The fight vanished from Russell's stance. "Canada?"

Tristan hadn't really meant to reveal that last bit. He'd just been so angry, the words had flown out. "You won't have to worry about what Saint Tristan thinks anymore."

"Tris," Russell breathed. "You can't be serious."

But he'd never been more serious about anything in his life. "Just love her, Russ. Or at least pretend like you do." Tristan heaved a sigh. "I'm tired. Both of you, see your way out."

"But, Tris," Russell tried.

"I have nothing left to say to you," Tristan bellowed, turning his attention from his brothers to his overturned wardrobe. "Just leave me be."

Phoebe collapsed on her bed, her shin throbbing from having taken a spill, rounding a corner in her attempt to catch Tristan. But he wasn't there. She'd seen no sign of him anywhere and if she'd known which chamber was his, she'd have sought him out there. Highly improper, but warranted in this case.

Alas, she didn't know which room was his and she couldn't open all of the doors in the family wing. She might stumble upon Russell, or worse, Lady Avery in doing so. No, she'd have to wait until morning. Blast it. Waiting was utter torture. But what other choice did she have?

She'd have to rise before dawn and plant herself in the breakfast room, then she'd stay there all morning, all day, if necessary. He'd have to make an appearance at some point and when he did, she'd make certain he heard her out. He said he loved her, after all. He'd listen to her, wouldn't he?

Of course then she'd have to deal with Russell. And her parents. And… Lady Avery. The latter struck more fear in her heart than all of the others combined. But Tristan had said he'd protect her. She had to believe he meant those words. She had to believe he loved her too.

The waiting was going to kill her. Phoebe's stomach roiled with unease and she turned on her side. Morning was only a few hours away. Just a few hours. She could wait that long, couldn't she?

Nineteen

WITH his bag slung over his shoulder and his right eye nearly closed shut, Tristan left the family wing. As he walked past his brother's study toward the garden doors, he heard Greg's voice. "Tristan."

He pinched the bridge over his nose to stave off an impending headache. But there was nothing for it. He'd probably never see Greg again. He supposed one last good-bye was in order. Tristan halted his step and backtracked to Greg's study. "Yes?" he said, poking his head in the door.

"God, you look awful." Though Greg was one to talk as he was still dressed in his clothes from the night before, with the exception of his cravat which lay in heap on his desk. "Have you broken your fast yet?"

Tristan shook his head. "Not hungry. I want to leave early. I'll get something along the road."

Greg sighed. "In that case, come in for a few

moments, will you?"

"Have you not gone to bed?" Tristan asked as he complied with his brother's request.

Greg shook his head. "You gave me a lot to think about last night, and I spent most of it reliving memories. Time must have gotten away from me." He gestured to a chair in front of his desk. "Sit."

Tristan didn't have time to sit. He certainly didn't want to bump into anyone else at Rufford Hall, and he didn't appreciate his brother keeping him from a speedy departure. "I'm headed out, Greg."

"Yes, never to return. I know." His oldest brother nodded, though it didn't seem as though he saw Tristan. "But with that being the case, I think you can give me a few moments, can't you?"

They'd never been particularly close, not like Tristan and Russell had once been. Still, they were brothers. "Yes, of course." Tristan dropped his bag on the floor, then crossed the room and sank into the seat.

Greg leaned forward in his chair, resting both of his elbows on his desk. "I want you to know I admire you, Tris. You're a better man than I am, a better man than Russ."

Where was this coming from? Tristan wasn't sure what to say, so he held his tongue, simply staring at his oldest brother.

"Marina was never truly mine. Even still I was never able to give her up," he muttered quietly.

Tristan managed to keep his mouth from dropping open. Greg had never broached this particular subject with him before. He'd never broached the subject with anyone before, as far as Tristan knew. It wasn't every day a man talked about cuckolding another one. "Why are you telling me this?"

"Because last night you did something I was never able to do."

Crashing his fist into Russell? No, Greg had never been the violent sort, but Tristan had, and Russell had deserved every punch that landed his way. He shrugged.

"I heard the love, the emotion in your voice last night. I remember when my own voice sounded that way." He smiled sadly.

Good God. How had Tristan sounded the night before? And what a bizarre conversation to be having with his oldest brother. "My voice?"

His brother speared him with his green Avery eyes. "But you love her enough to do the noble thing. To remove yourself from the equation. I never could have done that. If Marina was still—" he swallowed and a pained expression flashed on his face "—alive, I still wouldn't be able to do that. She was like some vice I couldn't escape. You're a better man than I am, Tristan, and I hope your life has a happier ending than mine has."

"Greg." Tristan sat forward in his chair. He wasn't sure what else to say. Marina Clayworth had been gone for years, but the pain of her loss could still be seen etched across his brother's face. "I don't think I'm all that noble. I never should have allowed myself to fall for her."

At that a self-deprecatory laugh escaped Greg. "Did you have control of it?"

Not in any way. Tristan shook his head.

"Neither did I." Then he sighed. "He'll treat her like he loves her, if I have to cut off his allowance and threaten to put a bullet in his skull."

Which was quite something coming from Greg, who only ever seemed to focus on himself. A lump formed in Tristan's throat, and once again he couldn't speak.

"She deserves you," Greg said softly. "But since that's not to be, I'll make sure he treats her well. Never fear about that."

Tears formed in Tristan's eyes. All he could do was nod, for fear that if he spoke he wouldn't be able to contain the emotion building inside him. He'd never see his brothers again. He'd never see his sister or her children. He'd never see Phoebe, but at least now he had Greg's word to see to her happiness. It was more than he could have hoped for when he awoke this morning.

"The coach is ready." Greg smiled sadly. "I won't ask you to stay because I know how difficult it must be for you to leave."

"Thank you," Tristan finally croaked out. For his words. For his candor. For his promise to see to Phoebe's care. Then he cleared his throat and rose from his seat. "For everything."

Greg pushed out of his chair and reached his hand out to Tristan, which was more affection than he'd ever received from his brother. "God speed," he said, clasping Tristan's hand a moment longer than was necessary, but which spoke volumes.

Fleetingly, Tristan wished he'd known Greg better, that they'd been closer, but on the precipice of his departure, he figured this was as close as they would ever be. "Take care," he said softly, then turned back toward the door and retrieved his bag. His coach, after all, awaited.

※

Phoebe was on her third cup of tea. Not that it mattered. She would drink ten pots if that's how long it took for Tristan to come down to breakfast. So far no one had made an appearance in the breakfast room, but as the sun began to filter in through the windows, she figured it wouldn't be much longer before someone did. She only prayed Tristan would appear before Russell did.

However it was Lord Avery that first strode into the room, looking as though he'd slept in his clothes the night before. Phoebe smiled a greeting at the baron. "Good morning, my lord."

"Good morning, Miss Greywood." A strange look flashed in the baron's eyes. Then he slid into a chair across from her. "You are up early this morning."

"I suppose I'm anxious to get a start on the day."

"Mmm. Brand new fresh day," the baron agreed, which was an odd thing for a man in yesterday's clothes to say, all things considered.

"Brand new fresh life," she replied.

"Indeed?" His brow lifted in surprise.

Just as soon as she could talk to Tristan, not that she could say as much to Lord Avery. Phoebe shrugged instead. "Are you headed to Leverton Park today, my lord?"

"No." He shook his head. "The few guests we have here is about the limit I can tolerate, no offense intended."

She supposed none was taken. Lord Avery was

certainly odd. His temperament wasn't like that of any of his siblings. He always struck her as more morose than the other Averys. "I admit I felt a little out of place there, myself, yesterday. If not for Cordie and Amelia and Tris… Lieutenant Avery, I wouldn't have fit in at all."

"Well, Russell will go over with you today. I'm certain you'll find your place among the ranks."

She didn't imagine Russell would want to take her anywhere after she called off their betrothal. Still she'd like to see Tristan first. "I'd hate to drag him away from whatever he'd rather do today. If Lieutenant Avery could be persuaded to escort me, I'm sure—"

"Tristan's gone, Miss Greywood."

"Gone?" Phoebe squeaked. She leapt to her feet and her chair fell backwards onto the floor.

Lord Avery's green eyes rounded in surprise. "About an hour ago, he headed back to London."

And then he'd head to Canada and Phoebe would never see him again. "But he can't have gone," she cried. Her head started to spin and her heart clenched. She had to see him. She had to tell him how she felt. Even if he left, even if he didn't feel the same, she had to tell him or she'd regret it the rest of her days.

Lord Avery rose to his feet. "He felt it was the for the best."

"He's wrong," she muttered, starting toward the corridor. An hour. She could still catch him. Possibly. "Was he riding?" If he was in a coach, she'd have a much better shot of reaching him.

"Certainly you don't mean to go after him." The baron looked aghast at the suggestion. "I don't imagine

Russell would appreciate that."

She didn't have time to argue with Lord Avery, and she didn't have time for propriety. Besides, it was the man's house, his stables she was going to need. "Please," she begged. "I've made a terrible error, my lord. I don't truly have time to explain, but if I don't reach Tristan, I'll lose him forever and I'll never forgive myself."

"You'll lose Tristan?" The baron frowned. "But you're betrothed to *Russell*."

Which was the error. Phoebe swiped at a tear. She didn't have time to cry. Not right now. "I was a coward, my lord. I didn't want this fortnight to be any more difficult than it already was. I should have told him upon my arrival that I had no intention of marrying him, but I didn't and now…"

"You need to go after Tristan," Lord Avery supplied. "Hurry. It's possible we can catch him."

"We?" Phoebe asked as she rounded the table, tripping on her hem; but she caught a chair and steadied her balance.

"We." The baron nodded, eyeing her with concern. "I swore to Tris I'd see to your care. Can you *ride*?"

She nodded quickly. "Better than I can walk."

"Come on then." He lifted his hand out to her. "We'd best hurry." He placed her hand in the crook of his arm and rushed her from the room and down the corridor, practically dragging her, not stopping when she stumbled, hurrying her along at a clip she could never manage on her own.

"Good heavens!" Lady Avery gasped, when she nearly collided with the pair. "What are you doing?" she asked.

"No time to talk, Mother," Lord Avery answered, as he guided Phoebe around the baroness toward the garden doors.

"Gregory Avery!" Lady Avery called after them, but they didn't stop.

They rushed through the garden, along the stone path to the stables. Lord Avery bellowed to the awaiting groomsmen, "My fastest two mounts, this instant."

"Have we got a sidesaddle?" one asked the other.

"Nay. Not since Lady Clayworth lived here."

The breath went out of Lord Avery. "A sidesaddle. My kingdom for a sidesaddle."

"I can ride astride," Phoebe called loudly, which was far from ladylike, but there truly wasn't time for delay.

Lord Avery's gaze shot to her. "You're hardly dressed for that, Miss Greywood."

"I can't lose him because of a saddle, my lord. Besides, I can ride faster astride."

"You truly do love him."

Phoebe nodded. "I only wish I'd realized it sooner."

"Very few of us get second chances. Relish yours." Then he turned his attention back to the groomsmen. "You heard the lady. She can ride astride. My fastest mounts in a thrice."

"Aye, my lord." The men rushed inside the stables, emerging moments later with two large hunters.

"You know you're going to have to deal with Russell?"

Phoebe nodded. "But we have to catch Tristan first."

Twenty

"TRISTAN! Tristan! Please stop!" Phoebe's voice echoed in Tristan's mind.

He'd apparently gone mad. Lack of sleep could do that to a man. He'd seen that more than once on the continent.

"Tristan!"

Or was he sleeping now? Dreaming of her calling his name from afar? If so, it was a bloody awful dream.

His heart still ached from her loss. If he was going to dream about her, he'd much rather dream about holding her again, about kissing her again, about tasting every inch of her skin.

"Morris, stop!" Greg's voice this time.

Greg's voice?

Tristan couldn't remember ever dreaming about his oldest brother, and certainly not in conjunction with Phoebe. He sat taller against the squabs and glanced out the coach window.

Good God!

No. He *must* to be dreaming. He had to be. Phoebe, with a daydress hiked up around her knees, sitting astride one of Greg's powerful hunters. And his brother a few feet away, a look of sheer determination on his face. If Tristan wasn't dreaming, he would kill Greg just as soon as he got his hands on him.

"Morris!" Tristan banged on the roof. "Stop."

The carriage slowed its pace, but before it came to a complete stop, Tristan tossed the door open and barged from the conveyance, fury and hope both pounding in his veins. "What the devil, Greg!" he demanded. "Have you lost your bloody mind?" He stalked toward the pair of horses that had also come to a stop. Tristan gestured to Phoebe with a wave of his hand. "You think putting *her* on a horse is seeing to her safety?"

Phoebe flushed red at the comment. "I am an expert horsewoman, Tristan Avery." Then apparently to prove her point, she tried to swing her leg over the hunter to dismount. But she wasn't wearing proper clothes and her bunched up dress got caught on the saddle and she slid over the side.

Tristan's heart clenched and his life flashed before his eyes. Faster than he knew he could move, he raced toward her, catching her just before she would have hit the ground.

Thank God.

His breathing labored, Tristan clutched her to him. He buried his face in her hair and kissed her head in relief. Her lilac scent enveloped him and Tristan was afraid to move, afraid that if he did or said anything that she'd turn to ash, that he'd realize he hadn't saved her after all.

But Phoebe's arms slid around his waist and she kissed his chest. "Oh, Tristan."

Hearing her voice made him breathe a bit easier. He pulled back slightly from her, gazing into her haunted azure eyes. "What are you doing here, Phoebe?"

"I came to stop you."

"Well, you've successfully done that. But why?" Why chase him across Nottinghamshire? Why risk her safety? And why the devil had Greg helped her?

Phoebe's eyes filled with tears. "You said you loved me. You said you always loved me."

Tristan tucked one of her loose auburn tendrils behind her ear and caressed her cheek with the back of his knuckles. "And you said you were too foxed to remember."

"I lied."

"I didn't." He couldn't help but smile at her, half embarrassed about the things he'd done, the things he'd said. "But I shouldn't have told you that. I shouldn't have—"

She stood up on her tiptoes, threw her arms around his neck, and pressed her lips to his. Tristan held her tight against him, reveling at the feel of her in his arms, pressed against his chest, the soft breaths that escaped her as she kissed him.

Her lips left his. Then she let her hands drift from his shoulders down his chest, pushing slightly back from him. "I'm so glad we found you."

Tristan stared at her in wonder, still not quite believing she was real. "I never thought I'd see you again."

A flash of ire lit her eyes as she lightly smacked his chest. "You have no one to blame but yourself for that. How could you run out on me?"

"Russell," he said in way of explanation. "I thought…"

"I've made a mess of everything, Tristan. But please don't leave. Please sort it out with me."

But she knew he couldn't do that. "I'm headed to Canada, Phoebe."

"Then take me with you."

Tristan's brow rose in surprise. She couldn't be serious. "You don't want to live in Canada."

"No." She shook her head. "I want to live in Norfolk, in Fairweather Cottage—"

"Fairweather Cottage?" he echoed.

"—And I want to live there with you," she continued as though he hadn't spoken. "But if takes going to Canada to have you, that's what I'll do, Tristan."

Did she really mean all of that? Tristan glanced from Phoebe to his brother, still astride a black hunter. Greg shrugged, casting Tristan a sly smile. "You could do worse, little brother."

But he could never do better. What Phoebe suggested was better than he could have ever hoped for.

※

Tristan quirked a grin at Phoebe that made her think she'd finally persuaded him. "You know this is madness?"

She did. All of it. Fleeing Rufford Hall. Racing across Notthinghamshire. Throwing every bit of caution to the wind. Phoebe nodded. "I love you."

Tristan heaved a sigh. "And I love you."

Her heart lifted, so relieved to hear those words from his lips. Phoebe beamed at him. "Then run away with me, Tristan. Let's turn your carriage around and let's race north."

"Elope?" He gaped at her and then glanced up at Lord Avery.

That sounded heavenly. And the perfect solution to their problems. They could race to Scotland, get married by an anvil preacher before her parents, his mother or Russell could complicate things further. They'd deal with all of that after they were man and wife. "Let's." She nodded once more. "Do you know what Cordie said to me yesterday?"

An amused expression settled on Tristan's face. "There is no telling."

"She said I should set my cap for the wrong fellow, but elope with the right one."

"Like she did?"

Phoebe nodded. He hadn't said no, not yet. "It worked for her."

"Go on," Lord Avery urged. "All your problems will still be waiting for you when you get back. You might not get another chance like this, and I can smooth things over with Mr. Greywood."

Perfect. The baron was on her side. Phoebe flashed him a thankful smile. What a lovely man he was—she'd had no idea until today. Then she turned her gaze back to Tristan. "You loved me enough to leave. Love me enough to run away with me."

"I love you with all my heart." He tilted his head toward the coach. "Climb in before Greg changes his mind."

But Phoebe didn't imagine Lord Avery would ever change his mind. For some reason he was her champion. For some reason it was important to him that she and Tristan find their happiness. And she wished that someday he'd find his own. She started for the carriage, but pain shot from her leg. She would have stumbled forward, but Tristan caught her about the waist.

"Should I prepare myself to carry you around the rest of our days?"

Phoebe smiled through her pain. "I think I twisted my leg when I fell from the saddle."

The smile on Tristan's face vanished. "Can you walk?"

She could hobble, but thought it best not to say that or he might change his mind about eloping. "A few days with it resting in a carriage will be perfect."

"Are you just saying that?" he asked suspiciously.

Phoebe nodded. "But it's very likely true."

Tristan leaned down and scooped her up in his arms. He glanced up at Lord Avery and said, "Tell her father I'll take care of her."

"You have my word."

The coachman opened the carriage door and just like the previous day, Tristan settled Phoebe on his lap. "Stretch your leg out on the bench, love."

Love. Phoebe sighed. She would never tire of hearing him say that word to her. She rested her head against Tristan's shoulder and let her fingers explore the gold buttons of his regimentals. Throbbing leg aside, she'd never been so content. "What did you do to your eye?" she asked.

"Just a scuffle, but I'm fine," he said as the coach lurched forward and then made a turn on the road, to head back north. "Now what is Fairweather Cottage?"

She tilted her head back to see him better. "Grandpapa said it was mine, if I wanted it. A nice little plot of land not far from Malvern Hall. It was part of my grandmother's dowry. My Uncle Simon was there for a while, but now he's at the hall with his wife and children."

"And you want to live there?"

She did. Phoebe smiled at him. "It's a rather good-sized cottage. I think we'd be happy there. I can't wait to show it to you."

"I think I'll be happy anywhere you are."

"Me too." She pressed her lips to his throat and smiled when he tightened his hold on her.

Twenty-One

CORDELIA, the Countess of Clayworth, gaped at her oldest brother. "I beg your pardon?" She must have misheard Gregory.

Her brother sat on the edge of her bed. "You heard me. They eloped. This very morning they started for Gretna Green."

"Phoebe and… *Tristan*?" Cordie shook her head. Not that the news didn't make her happy. Tristan was her dearest brother and Phoebe was one of her dearest friends, but she was fairly certain up until two minutes ago that the pair actively disliked each other.

Greg nodded. "I thought it best if you broke the news to everyone."

"You did, did you?" Cordie folded her arms across her chest. Normally, she wouldn't have minded doing that very thing, but the news had completely dumbfounded her.

"It was your suggestion, from what I understand." It

appeared as though Greg was biting back a smile. Blast him. Cordie hated being the second to know something, and she certainly hated Greg's delight over the situation.

"I suggested no such thing."

Greg heaved a sigh, though his green eyes twinkled mischievously, which was odd for him. "I heard her say so with my own ears, Cordie. You told her to set her cap for the wrong man, but to elope with the right one."

Cordie clamped her mouth shut. She had said those very words. Just yesterday. But how was she to know *Tristan* was the right one?

"Besides," Greg continued, enjoying himself rather a lot, "I think Russ will take the news better coming from you than anyone else."

"Do you?"

Greg shrugged. "And I don't think he'd hit an expectant woman."

Cordie glared at her oldest brother. "But he'd most certainly hit you."

"I did give them my coach and my blessing."

Then he deserved to be hit. "Coward."

Greg winked at her. "They're all down in Moore's drawing room."

Cordie shook her head. "I'm afraid Brendan doesn't want me to leave this bed, Greg. You'll have to tell them yourself."

He leaned forward and tweaked her nose. "You don't really mean that. Only you can soothe the Greywoods' ruffled feathers. Only you can make Russell accept the situation with a word or two. You're so much better at managing everyone than I am."

"Flattery will get you everywhere," Cordie

grumbled, though she couldn't help smiling at Greg. "Are they truly happy?"

Greg nodded. "You should have seen them, Cordie. She bolted across Nottinghamshire as though the devil chased us. I've never seen a girl ride so fast. I've never seen a girl, other than you, so determined before. And when we finally reached him, I wish you could have seen his face." He frowned. "Well, after he berated me for putting her in danger. But when she kissed him, all the darkness that's been so much a part of him lately was gone. He was like Tristan was before he left for war. Full of hope. Full of life." Greg smiled. "He loves her so very much."

Greg's words made a lump form in Cordie's throat. How could she be angry with Tristan or Phoebe for following their hearts, even if she was the one who had to explain it to their families? Then a joyous thought popped in her mind. "And we'll still be sisters."

"There is that," Greg agreed. "And she is persuasive. If I had to put a wager on it, I'd say she completely talked him out of the whole Canada nonsense."

"Canada?" Cordie rubbed her brow. What else had she missed?

"Don't worry about it. I don't believe they're going now."

"To Canada?" Cordie sputtered. "No, no one is going to Canada, not if I have anything to say about it. Good heavens!"

"Don't get all worked up. You have a room full of people downstairs who are waiting for you."

Cordie glared at her oldest brother one last time. "Gregory Avery, you will pay for this."

He grinned like he used to, back when they were children. "I am certain you'll try."

―⋆⋅☆⋅⋆―

"You haven't seen Phoebe?" Russell asked Amelia in the corner of the drawing room.

"Not since yesterday," the blonde replied.

"Greg said she'd already come over here." Which Russell had found odd that she'd leave on her own without an escort. "You don't think she's up in Cordie's room, do you?"

"I was up there not long ago, Russell. If she was there, she was hiding under the bed."

Which was almost exactly what Russell had suggested to Tristan the previous night. Before their scuffle. Before Greg interfered. Before the world had stopped making sense. "Did Tristan come by before he started for London?" Perhaps his brother had taken the opportunity to spend one last morning with Phoebe, escorting her to Leverton Park.

"If he did, I didn't see him," Amelia replied. "What's wrong, Russell? You don't quite look yourself."

He probably didn't. It wasn't every day, after all, that you found out your bother was in love with your fiancée. An emptiness settled in Russell's belly. He'd known that he and Tris had grown apart, but he always figured they'd find their way back to each other once the dust of war and returning home had settled. But they never would be the same again. How could they? He was going to marry the girl Tristan loved, and his brother would never forgive him for it. How the devil had they found themselves in this situation? "Didn't sleep well last night," he replied truthfully. He wondered if he would ever sleep well again.

"Chamomile tea," Amelia suggested. "Philip drinks it nearly every night."

"Ah!" Mrs. Greywood gushed. "Lady Clayworth, you are glowing."

The drawing room fell to a hush as Russell and the others all turned their attention to Cordie, who stood just inside the doorway. She wore the strangest expression, as though she was frightened, which wasn't like Cordie in the least.

"Thank you, Mrs. Greywood. I'm so glad to see you," Cordie said, more quietly than she normally should have. Then she swallowed nervously.

Good God. Was something wrong? With Cordie? Or with the child? Russell's heart constricted.

"I…um…Well, I have some news you all need to hear," Cordie continued, though her eyes had settled on Russell. "It's about Phoebe."

"Phoebe?" Mrs. Greywood gasped. "Has something happened?"

"Nothing bad," Cordie hastened to explain. An overly cheerful smile, which seemed feigned, settled on her face. "She's… eloped."

Russell staggered backwards a bit.

"Eloped?" Mr. Greywood roared.

"Oh, don't be angry," Cordie begged, putting her hand in the air as though that would halt the man's anger. "She is very happy and I know she'll want all of you to be happy as well."

Mrs. Greywood grasped her husband's arm as though to steady herself. "Eloped?" she echoed.

"I'm sure it will come as a surprise to you, as much

as it did to me. I had no idea Tristan and Phoebe were so very much in love, but…"

Tristan! Russell's head spun just a bit. Tristan had stolen his fiancée? No, Russell's earlier estimation was quite true. He and his brother would never find their way back to each other. How could they after this?

―――

How Greg thought she could soothe Russell, Cordie had no idea. She'd never seen Russ look so murderous. Luckily, Greg started toward the Greywoods, offering his congratulations and assuring them Phoebe would be a welcome member of the family.

But that left Russell to Cordie. She gulped as she crossed the drawing room, where Amelia had her hand on Russell's arm.

"Russ," Cordie whispered. "Do you need to sit down?"

"No," he spat out. "I need to get my hands on my little brother."

He was going to be difficult, even after the way he'd neglected Phoebe and treated her so poorly these last several months. Cordie frowned at Russell. "Why don't we take a walk in the garden?"

"So you can get me away from all of these people?"

Cordie shook her head. "Because I think the fresh air would be good for both of us."

He shook his head. "I could still catch them."

"And do what?" Cordie's green eyes sought his. "I know you don't want to hear this, Russ. But all of this is for the best. Can't you see?"

"I see that my fiancée was stolen from me."

"If you'd truly cared about her, you should have

treated her better, Russell. You could have married her long before now, but you were too busy seeking your own pursuits."

Her brother gaped at her. "I beg your pardon?"

Cordie scoffed. Certainly he wasn't going to pretend innocence. "She was perfectly aware of what you were doing in Town this summer, as was I. She was waiting to call off the betrothal until the end of the fortnight at Rufford Hall."

Russell's countenance darkened. "She planned this all along?"

That Cordie doubted, but she wasn't at all certain what to say. "You don't want to be married and you don't want to be married to her. So consider yourself lucky that you made an escape. I, for one, am happy that my friend will have a husband who cares for her."

"And you don't care that she's made a fool out of me?"

"You are my brother and I love you, Russ," Cordie said. And no matter what sort of scoundrel he was half the time, she did love him. "Brendan and I are headed to Bayhurst Court in less than a week. He's anxious about my condition."

Russell said nothing, just stared blankly at her.

"Why don't you come with us? Don't go back to London. Don't stay here. Come spend the autumn with us."

"I—" he shook his head "—I don't know, Cordie."

"You know you love Derbyshire. Mother won't be there and…"

Finally he nodded. "Let me think about it. A change of scenery might be good for me."

Twenty-Two

"Scotland is freezing!" Phoebe shivered as they entered the White Heather Inn.

Tristan chuckled, directing her past the innkeeper and toward the staircase that lead to their chamber. "I suppose it's a good thing we aren't headed to Canada then."

Phoebe stopped in her tracks, rose up on her tiptoes and pressed a kiss to her husband's lips. "I would have gone, Tristan."

"And shivered and chattered your teeth and been miserable."

But that wasn't true. Phoebe shook her head. "Not as long as you were there." Of that she had never been more certain. If she'd had any question about that, the sennight they'd spent on the road north had only made her more confident about her decision. Tristan took care with her. He made sure she was comfortable and happy. And he kissed her senselessly.

"Oh?"

Phoebe grinned at him as she turned the overly large Avery crest ring around her finger with her thumb. "You'd keep me warm."

"Mmm." A rakish grin lit his lips. "I'm about to keep you warm in Scotland." Then he placed his hand at the small of her back and urged her toward the steps that led to their rented room.

His touch coupled with his words sent warmth shooting to her core. She'd waited, fairly impatiently, for this night. Ever the gentleman, Tristan had secured separate rooms along their journey until now. She hastened her pace, but he caught her around the waist, pulling her back to his front. "Walk with care, Mrs. Avery." His voice rumbled over her like a caress.

She slid her hands over his and squeezed his fingers. "I didn't even stumble, Lieutenant."

"I'd rather not take the chance," he said, scooping her up in his arms.

Phoebe let out a squeal of surprise, but she draped her arms around his neck as she started for the staircase. "Do walk with care, sir," she teased him.

Tristan's brow rose in amusement. "Oh, such a clever mouth you have." Then he jostled her slightly as she jingled the handle to their room and pushed it open. After stepping over the threshold, he let her slide down his front until her feet found purchase on the rug. "Here, let me kiss it." Then he dipped his head down to hers and captured her mouth, suckling her bottom lip, sending desire shooting to her core.

He lifted his head, grinning as though he knew exactly what he did to her. Phoebe could do nothing but grin right back.

"Turn around," he ordered, spinning her away from him. Then his fingers worked on the fastenings of her dress. Each bit of skin he revealed, Tristan pressed his lips there until her dress finally pooled at her feet. He fingered the ribbon straps of her chemise before untying them.

Phoebe clutched her chemise to her chest, keeping it from following her dress to the floor.

"Come now." Tristan's lips pressed against the side of her neck and his hands drifted over her shoulders, brushing over her breasts to take her hands in his. "Let me see all of you, love."

His thumbs caressed her nipples, making them ache against her chemise. Then he urged her hands away from her chest and the silk slid down her body. Tristan's hands returned to her breasts, reverently circling her nipples.

"Mmm." He pinched them, making the ache between Phoebe's legs grow. "Does that feel good?"

Unable to speak, she nodded.

He nipped her shoulder, then let his hands drift lower to the top of her drawers. "Take these off and get into bed."

Bed. Phoebe gulped, but her eyes immediately found the small bed on the other side of the room. Good heavens. She thought she was ready for this. She'd been wishing for this night since they'd first set out from Nottinghamshire.

She was ready for this. She was with Tristan and she wanted this. Phoebe stepped from her slippers, padded across the rug, then slid her drawers down her legs.

Good heavens! They were damp!

Phoebe climbed onto the bed and slid under the counterpane as Tristan shrugged out of his jacket, a look of admiration in his eyes. He tossed his jacket to a nearby chair and then yanked his shirt over his head. He crossed the floor, sat on the edge of their bed and pulled his boots from his feet, dropping both to the floor with dull thuds.

Then he was beside her, atop the counterpane, while she was beneath it. Phoebe's mouth went dry as she looked at him, the expanse of his bare shoulders, the light dusting of dark hair on his chest, the muscles she wanted to explore with her fingers and her lips.

"Still hiding from me?" One of Tristan's eyebrows rose in amusement. "Do you know how long I've wanted to look upon you?"

"Always?" she quipped and then wished she hadn't when her cheeks warmed.

Tristan chuckled. "Always, indeed." His hand flattened across her belly, then he grabbed a handful of the counterpane and pulled it downward until her breasts were bared for him. He licked his lips. "I've always wanted to taste you too." Then he lowered his head to one of her straining nipples and sucked it into his mouth.

Phoebe sucked in a breath. Desire pooled lower and lower in her belly, and she thought she might shoot off the bed when his rough tongue flicked across her nipple. His fingers found her other nipple and he plucked and pinched her until she was squirming beneath the counterpane.

Tristan shifted on the bed until he was over her,

straddling her legs caught beneath the counterpane. He kissed his way to her neck, across her jaw and then to her ear. "I'm going to make you mine."

The promise sent shivers racing down her spine. Phoebe smiled and tentatively touched his back, reveling in the feel of his muscles beneath her fingertips. "Make me yours, Tristan."

His lips sought hers as he rolled to the side, bringing her with him until she lay atop him and her naked bottom was in the air. His hand found her backside and he lightly spanked her. "No more hiding."

Phoebe's mouth dropped open in surprise.

"I do like that look on you," he said rakishly. Then he kissed her once more. "Now lay on your back."

She scrambled back to her spot on the bed, lying completely bare.

"Stiff as a board," he said. "I'm going to have to loosen you up."

Phoebe gulped and her heart pounded so loudly it echoed in her ears. Tristan pushed her knees apart and gazed at her most secret place. Appreciation lit his eyes and a ragged breath escaped her.

"Relax, love," he crooned as he tentatively brushed his hand through her damp curls and one questing finger pressed inside her. Dear Heavens, it was… it was the most amazing thing she'd ever felt.

She sucked in a breath at his sensual intrusion. Relax. Ha! She thought she might splinter into pieces right then and there. "Tristan," she breathed out.

"Shh," he whispered before leaning forward and placing a kiss inside her right thigh. "I'll be gentle."

His finger at her core pressed deeper and his breath

on her leg heated her more than she'd known was possible. His finger left her, only to enter her once again a moment later as he set a rhythm with the motion that left her more than breathless. His continual plunge and retreat stoked a fire within her and Phoebe feared she might burst into flames right then and there. So much for Scotland being cold.

"So wet." His voice sounded lower, more gravely, and Phoebe's stomach fluttered at the sound. Tristan's green depths locked with her gaze and a seductive grin settled on his lips. "Beautiful, Phoebe. You're so beautiful."

Then he hooked her right leg over his shoulder and leaned forward, closer and closer to her core until his lips found her center. His warm tongue slid inside her and another gasp was wrenched from Phoebe's soul.

Tristan chuckled, but less than a moment later, he resumed his ministrations. His tongue circled a little nub and then he sucked it into his mouth.

"Tristan!" She didn't even recognize her own voice, so husky and passion laden.

He kissed her core once more then licked her with more fervor, going faster and deeper and…

"More," she whispered.

Which was the wrong thing to do, as he lifted his head and stopped his sensual torture altogether. "I thought you'd never ask."

Never ask? Her foggy mind tried to make sense of his words, but then she saw what he meant. Tristan leaned backward and undid the fastenings of his trousers. And then… And then…

Phoebe's mouth went dry at that sight of him. Dear

heavens, he was… Well, there was quite a lot to him. Fingers and tongues were one thing but that… "Tristan, I don't think," she began.

"Don't think," he urged and tossed his trousers across the room. His gaze met hers and seemed to promise something. "Don't think, Phoebe. Just let me love you."

He pushed her knees further apart and settled himself between them. Then he placed his hands on either side of her head, leaned forward and captured her lips. His kiss, so tender, so hot, made her moan from want. When his tongue swept inside her mouth to tangle with hers, Phoebe thought she would melt right into the bedclothes.

Tristan lowered himself down to his elbows and pressed her further into the mattress, his strong, muscled chest flush against her breasts. His lips left hers to trail across her jaw, then they lingered by her ear. "I'm going to fill you, Phoebe. And then you'll be mine."

She never wanted anything else in her life as much as she wanted what he promised in that moment. The tip of his manhood prodded her opening, stretching her more than his fingers had done. "Oh!" she said.

His lips still by her ear, he whispered. "It's all right, my love. I'll take care of you. Now and always."

He pushed himself further inside her and Phoebe closed her eyes, unable to do anything other than feel the length of him stretching her more and more with each inch he took. Then he stopped.

Her eyes flew open. "What?" she asked, her breath coming out in pants.

"It may hurt." He frowned. "But just this once."

It felt too good to hurt. "Please," she begged him to continue.

Then he thrust forward, filling her completely. The pain was sharp and Phoebe gasped, but it was gone a moment later and then all she could feel was Tristan seated deeply within her.

"I'm sorry," he said, his green eyes seeking her reassurance.

She shook her head. "It's over now. Please don't stop."

He lowered his head once more, kissing her softly as he moved within her, then he found the same rhythm his fingers had moments earlier. He thrust and retreated and thrust again, pushing Phoebe toward a precipice she didn't understand but craved more than her next breath.

His speed increased. He anchored her hands with his, pressing faster and deeper until she fell over the precipice, calling out his name. Wave after wave of release washed over her and then Tristan cried out with his own release.

He collapsed onto the bed and cradled her against him, his hands caressing her side and back, his lips kissing the top of her head. "Dear God, Phoebe."

There wasn't a word to describe how amazing that was. So Phoebe simply ran her fingers through the dark hair on his chest and nuzzled against him.

Twenty-Three

PHOEBE'S hair tickled Tristan's nose and he woke up with a jolt. Morning light was just beginning to filter into the room, dancing off his wife's pretty backside. There was something to be said for making love to the woman you loved. After experiencing the most amazing night of his life, he felt bad for any man who never got to experience such a thing.

Phoebe moaned softly and snuggled closer to him. Tristan pulled the counterpane up to cover her and draped his arm around Phoebe, not able to stop himself from caressing her soft, ivory skin. Her hand clutched the counterpane and the sunlight reflected off the too-large ring on her finger. He'd have to get her something more appropriate once they reached civilization. But yesterday it had been the best he had to offer.

After a moment, Phoebe lifted her head; her dark tresses spilled over her shoulders, pooling on his chest. "Good morning," she said groggily.

"You can go back to sleep, love," he said, staring into her sleepy azure eyes.

But she shook her head and the movement of her hair tickled his chest. "We need to start for home."

Home. Where was that? "Norfolk?" he asked.

She grinned. "Grandpapa will love you."

Tristan wasn't so sure about that. Viscount Malvern would most likely not love the man who'd absconded with his granddaughter, no matter how much he loved her. "I'll settle for him liking me."

"What do you think about heading to Bayhurst Court first, though?"

"Bayhurst Court?" he echoed. Where had that come from?

"Cordie and Clayworth should be home by now. I—" she shrugged slightly as one of her hands smoothed across his chest "—Well, I'd like to see her and explain. She's my dearest friend."

Tristan agreed with a nod. "If that's what you want, love."

Phoebe leaned forward and brushed her lips against his. "I love you."

"I'll never tire of hearing that."

※

The road to Derbyshire was wet and muddy most of the way, but Phoebe didn't care and she was relatively sure Tristan didn't either. Wrapped in each other's arms, Phoebe was never cold.

When a sandstone Tudor manor could be seen against the rolling backdrop of Derbyshire, Tristan sat tall and heaved a sigh. Was he nervous? Phoebe slid her hand across his chest. "Are you all right?"

He nodded. "Did you know when Cordie and Clayworth returned from their elopement, Greg, Russ, Mother and I were all here waiting for them?"

"She never mentioned that."

"Oh, I'm sure she didn't. Greg and Clayworth butted heads immediately. And Mother was awful and Clayworth ordered her from the house." Tristan frowned. "I haven't been back since."

"Clayworth ordered your mother from Bayhurst Court?" It was a wonder Cordie hadn't mentioned that, not that her friend was ever keen to discuss her mother.

"They've never spent the night under the same roof since."

"I'm not surprised," Phoebe said.

Her husband turned full attention to her. "Why would you say that?"

She'd promised Cordie never to reveal her secret to anyone, but Tristan wasn't just anyone. He was Cordie's brother, Phoebe's husband. "They were newly married, like we are. You've seen every inch of me."

Tristan nodded, though the expression in his eyes made it clear he had no idea what she was talking about.

"He had to have seen her scars, and you know how much he loves her."

"Scars?" Tristan echoed.

Phoebe couldn't meet his eyes anymore and her gaze dropped to her lap. "I only saw them once, and there were fresh wounds at the time too."

"Phoebe, what are you saying?"

She shook her head. "Her back is covered in scars, Tristan. Wounds your mother inflicted."

"Oh my God." The breath rushed out of Tristan. For

the longest time he said nothing and then whispered, "I had no idea."

"How could you? You were off fighting in wars." She finally met his eyes. "She didn't blame you for not being there."

"Mother was harsh when we were children, but…" Tristan clasped her hands in his. "That's why you're afraid of my mother."

There was no use denying it. Phoebe nodded. "I don't want to be around her. I don't want to subject our children to her, not without one of us present at all times."

"Good God." He shook his head. "You sound just like Clayworth did. I can't even imagine how bad Cordie's back must look."

He didn't want to know. Phoebe would never get the image out of her own mind. "She made me swear never to tell anyone."

"I won't tell her I know," he promised, though Phoebe could hear the pain in his voice.

"I'm sorry. I shouldn't have told you."

"No. I don't want you to keep secrets from me. I just wish I'd known before. That Cordie had confided in me." He shook his head. "That's why she was so determined to chase after Haversham and why you helped her."

Phoebe nodded.

The color drained from Tristan's face. "And then I threatened to *horsewhip* you? Oh God, Phoebe." He cupped her face in his hands. "I would never do that. I would never hurt you."

She kissed his hands. "I know. I know that."

He leaned forward and kissed her brow. "I'm so sorry if I frightened you back then."

He had, but she knew it wasn't who he truly was. Phoebe leaned into him, resting her head against his chest. "All is forgotten, Tristan. All is forgiven."

His arms wrapped around her and Phoebe closed her eyes, wishing she hadn't inflicted this pain on him.

Soon, the carriage came to a stop, and they waited for the coachman to open the door. Tristan alighted from the conveyance and then offered his hand to Phoebe, drawing her out onto the circled drive.

"Come along, Mrs. Avery." Tristan smiled at her. "Let's go explain ourselves to the earl and countess, shall we?"

Together they walked the path to the front door. Tristan knocked and a moment later, the door opened and a butler ushered them over the threshold.

"Lieutenant Avery," the man said in surprise.

"Fielding." Tristan nodded. "I'm hoping my sister is in residence."

"Indeed, sir."

"Perfect. Will you inform her that my wife and I have arrived?"

"If you'll wait in the white parlor, Lieutenant, I'll inform the countess."

But Russell's voice came from the far end of the corridor. "How very surprising to find you here," the captain growled.

Good God. The last person in the world Tristan expected to bump into at Bayhurst Court was his brother. His mind was still reeling after hearing the awful tale about his mother and Cordie.. Tristan was ill prepared to see his brother at the moment. He knew he'd have to face Russell eventually, but he hadn't planned on eventually happening so soon. "I could say the same about you," he replied.

"Lady Clayworth is in the nursery, Fielding," Russell barked, increasing his stride until he stood before Tristan and Phoebe. "I'll entertain my *brother* and his wife until you fetch her."

"Very good, Captain." The butler bustled from front foyer as though his clothes were on fire.

Phoebe tightened her hold on Tristan's arm as though she was terrified. He glanced down at her, hoping to offer her a bit of comfort. Russell was clearly furious, but he'd never harm her. That wasn't in his brother's nature, but knowing what their mother was capable of, her fear was certainly founded. "I owe you an explanation, Russ," Tristan said calmly. "Why don't we go outside and talk?"

"An explanation?" Russell scoffed. "I'd say that's the least you owe me." Then he gestured to the front parlor with an exaggerated sweep of his hand. "Do come in, Lieutenant and Mrs. Avery, I am dying to hear what you've been up to."

Tristan sighed. "There's no need to do this in front of Phoebe, Russ." Besides they could both be more candid if it was just the two of them.

"Well, she's part of this too, isn't she? My brother and *my* fiancée?"

A patter of hurried footsteps sounded down the corridor and then a very feminine gasp. "Tristan!" Cordie hurried forward, panic lacing her voice. "What are you doing here?"

Tristan dragged his eyes from Russell to their sister. "Phoebe wanted to see you before we started for Norfolk. Why don't you take her to go see Julian? Russell and I have some catching up of our own to do."

"No, no, no, no, no." Cordie shook her head. "I won't have the two of you killing each other."

"Who says we'll both die?" Russell asked.

Cordie huffed indignantly. "Russell Avery, go to your chambers."

"Like a chastened schoolboy?" Russ shook his head. "You're not my mother, Cordie, but if Tristan is so keen to have this be between just the two of us, I'll take that walk he first suggested."

Thank God. Tristan pried Phoebe's fingers from his arm. "Go with Cordie, love. I'll be back soon."

Her azure eyes welled up with tears and Tristan ached to wrap his arms around her and soothe her, but that wasn't to be at the moment. Not with Russell looking on with his murderous expression.

Tristan glanced back at his brother and gestured to the door at his back. "After you, Russ."

※

Phoebe thought her heart would break when Tristan followed Captain Avery out the front door. But then Cordie threw her arms around Phoebe and squeezed her tight.

"What have you done, Phoeb?" her friend whispered.

"Followed my heart." She sniffed back tears.

Cordie stepped back from her. "I never would have thought that would lead you to Tristan." She smiled a watery smile. "Come. Let's wait in the parlor."

Phoebe shook her head. "Should we just let them go off like that?"

Cordie snorted. "We certainly can't stop them. I'm just glad neither of them has a pistol on them." Then she frowned. "Tristan doesn't have a pistol, does he?"

Not that Phoebe knew about. "Maybe in the carriage?"

"Morris won't let them do something that foolish." Cordie linked her arm with Phoebe and towed her toward the closest parlor on the left. "We'll wait in here and you can tell me all about your mad dash north."

Just as they were about to step into the parlor, Lord Clayworth's voice came from the other end of the corridor. "Fielding said Tristan…" He stopped in his tracks when his eyes landed on Phoebe. "Fielding was correct." Then a genuine smile lit his lips. "Miss…that is…Mrs. Avery, you're looking well."

"Thank you, my lord."

"Brendan," Cordie began, "Tris and Russell have gone outside to beat each other senseless. Will you make certain they don't kill each other?"

The earl heaved a sigh and then shook his head. "Nor do I plan to step into the middle of a pack of rabid dogs. They'll work it out better if I don't interfere."

"But—"

"No buts." Lord Clayworth gestured Cordie and Phoebe into the parlor. "We'll wait in here."

Cordie tugged Phoebe toward a settee and then pulled her down beside her. "How was Scotland?" she asked, turning her full attention to Phoebe.

"Cold." Or it had been until Tristan made certain she was warm.

"And so now we're sisters, after all." Cordie smiled. "I am glad about that, Phoebe."

But not glad about the way it all happened. Phoebe could see it etched across her friend's face. "We shouldn't have come. Cordie, I'm sorry. I asked Tristan to bring me here, so I could explain everything to you. I had no idea Captain Avery would be here."

"I thought it best if Russ came here instead of heading back to Town." Cordie squeezed Phoebe's hand. "You couldn't have guessed he'd be here. And you don't owe me an explanation. You've always been a loyal and dear friend, and you'll always have my loyalty in return."

There truly wasn't anyone as loyal as Cordelia Clayworth.

"Besides," Lord Clayworth put in, "Gregory Avery already told us everything. Your mad dash to catch Tristan. How in love the two of you are." His dark blue eyes seemed to assess Phoebe as though he wasn't quite certain who she was any longer. "Cordie and I could never fault you for that. In fact, I think you're rather brave to have taken your future in hand the way you did."

"Thank you," Phoebe replied. "I don't feel brave." Though it was kind of him to try and make her feel better.

"So what are your plans?" Cordie asked. "Greg said something about Norfolk, but then he said something about Canada, and Philip said something about Tristan transferring to the 16th and…"

Phoebe smiled at her friend. "The plan is Norfolk."

"Brilliant." Cordie grinned. "Especially as I forbade

Philip from sending off some glowing letter of recommendation Tristan had asked him for. Canada, for heaven's sakes."

Which echoed Phoebe's thoughts exactly. "Grandpapa offered Fairweather Cottage to me several months ago. I'd like to be close to my parents." Then she paused, half afraid of how to ask the next question, but she had to know. "Are they furious with me?"

"Stunned." Cordie shook her head. "But we all were. They seem to have accepted the situation though, and Matthew seemed rather happy about the whole thing."

Of course, Matthew never had cared for Russell. Phoebe glanced back toward the corridor. "You don't really think they'll beat each other senseless, do you?"

Cordie snorted. "Men and their propensity for hitting things and each other."

"You just don't understand the male mind, *ma minouche.*" Clayworth winked at his wife.

"No," she agreed. "I tend to think situations can be better solved with words than with fists."

❧

Tristan followed Russell toward Bayhurst's elaborate garden until his brother turned around, hatred flashing in his eyes. "So explain, Tris. Explain how you stole my fiancée. I am all ears."

"I understand you're angry, Russ."

"You understand, do you?" His brother scoffed. "Because I'm having a difficult time understanding any of this."

And, honestly, Tristan had no idea how to explain it. "You never loved her," he said instead.

"That is beside the point. She was my fiancée. And

you were my brother and my best friend."

Tristan shook his head. "No. That's entirely the point, Russell. I love her. I love her with every beat of my heart, and she loves me."

"Every beat of your heart? Who do you think you are? Byron with that drivel?"

"If you ever meet the girl for you, Russ, you'll understand."

"No, I don't think I will." Russell's eyes narrowed even further, his jaw stiff as though he was barely containing his fury. "I would never have betrayed you. And there's not a thing you can say to justify your doing so to me."

Perhaps he was right, but Tristan would make the same choice all over again. Living without Phoebe had been torturous, and watching Russell make a fool of her had only been more so. Tristan heaved a sigh. "Then I hope someday you can forgive me, Russ."

"And I hope to never see you again."

Well, that was perfectly clear, wasn't it? Tristan nodded. "Then I'll just retrieve my wife and be on my way." Then he turned on his heel and started back for the manor house.

He found Phoebe, Cordie and Clayworth inside the front parlor, and as he entered the room, Phoebe leapt to her feet.

"Are you all right?" She rushed to his side.

He would be eventually, and he'd be better once they left Derbyshire. Tristan draped his arm around Phoebe's shoulder and then turned his attention to his sister. "I'm afraid Phoebe and I can't stay. We truly must start for Norfolk."

Cordie didn't look surprised when she smiled sadly at him. "He'll come around eventually."

But Tristan doubted that, not that he could do anything about it one way or the other. He would miss Russell, with whom he'd spent nearly every day of his life, but they had grown apart the last year. They weren't the same as they'd once been, and now they never would be. "Well, that's entirely up to him." He nodded at his brother-in-law. "Good to see you, Clayworth. Take care of my sister, will you?"

"Until the end of time."

Which was all anyone could ever ask, wasn't it? Tristan wrapped Phoebe's hand around his arm and led her back outside to their awaiting coach.

"I'm sorry," Phoebe muttered once they were back on the road, headed south.

Tristan tucked her against him. "Don't be. Given the chance, I'd make the same choices, Phoebe. You're all I've ever wanted in life, and I'll love you until the end of time."

Epilogue

Fairweather Cottage, Norfolk – February 1816

PHOEBE stared at the unopened letter in her hand as though it was adder, poised to strike her. She knew Captain Avery's hand as well as she knew her own husband's. After all these months, what could Russell possibly have to say to Tristan?

A boisterous laughter filled the corridor outside the sitting room and Phoebe rose to her feet. A moment later, Tristan and Matthew filed into the room, grinning from ear to ear. Phoebe tucked the letter into her pocket and eyed the two men suspiciously. "You only laugh," she said to her brother, "when you're up to something."

"You're so distrustful, Phoeb." Her brother winked at her.

That was it. The two of them were up to something. Matthew never winked, he'd also never tell her anything she wanted to know. So Phoebe tilted her head to the side and grinned at her husband. "Tristan."

Her brother laughed louder than he had in the corridor. "God help me if a woman should ever look at me like that, Avery."

"If she does," Tristan said, "you should hold on to her forever." Then he crossed the floor, tipped Phoebe's chin upward and pressed his warm lips to hers. "Miss me?"

"Always."

Matthew gagged. "On that note, I think I'll get back to the Hall." Then he pointed his finger at Tristan. "But don't you tell her a thing."

"On my honor."

Whatever their secret was, Tristan would spill it the moment Matthew left the cottage.

"Oh, and Grandfather has requested your presence for dinner tomorrow night."

"Yes, he sent a note this morning. Tristan and I will be there," she promised.

Then Phoebe waited until her brother left and the front door signaled his departure from Fairweather before she rose up on her tiptoes and pressed her lips once more to Tristan's. "What aren't you supposed to tell me?"

He chuckled, lightly smacking her behind. "Did you not hear me promise on my honor?"

"But you don't believe in secrets between the two of us."

Tristan shook his head. "An exception I make when someone's birthday is around the corner."

A birthday secret. She simply had to know now.

"Don't even think to persuade me. I can withstand any temptation you can throw my way, Mrs. Avery. I'm a decorated war hero, I'll have you know."

Phoebe bit back a smile. She'd have the truth out of him in seconds. "I've been so cold today, Tristan," she said, running her fingers across his chest.

His green eyes narrowed. "You are shameless."

She was no longer able to hold back a grin when he scooped her up in his arms, but the crinkle of the letter in her pocket caught his notice.

"What's that?" he asked.

Now she'd never get the truth out of him. Phoebe reached into her pocket and retrieved the Captain's letter. "Oh, this came for you today."

He carried her over to the settee and sat. She stayed on his lap, leaning her head against his chest while he opened the letter.

When all he said was, "Hmm," Phoebe sat taller and met his eyes.

She was afraid to ask, but had to know. "Well, what did he say?"

"Not much." Tristan frowned, but he handed the note to her.

Tristan,
You were right.
Russell

Phoebe blinked at her husband. "What are you right about?"

He shook his head. "I'm not sure. But in the last conversation we had, I told him if he ever found the right girl, he'd understand why we did what we did. Perhaps some chit has finally caught him in her clutches."

"Ladies don't like to be thought of as having clutches."

"Hmm." Tristan kissed her brow. "But you have them just the same. And I'm so very happy to be caught in yours."

About the Author

AVA STONE is a USA Today bestselling author of Regency historical romance and college age New Adult romance. Whether in the 19th Century or the 21st, her books explore deep themes but with a light touch. A single mother, Ava lives outside Raleigh NC, but she travels extensively, always looking for inspiration for new stories and characters in the various locales she visits.

Feel free to visit her at:
www.avastoneauthor.com
www.desolatesun.com

Printed in Great Britain
by Amazon